THE DETECTIVES MATE

CASSANDRA DOON

CASEY ROLLS

"Be with me always - take any form - drive me mad! Do not leave me in this abyss where I cannot find you! Oh, God! it is unutterable! I can not live without my life! I can not live without my soul!"
— Emily Brontë, Wuthering Heights

PROLOGUE
4 MONTHS EARLIER

My body went rigid, the blood in my veins turning to ice. My heart felt like it had stopped altogether, a heavy weight pressing down on my chest—the need for oxygen burned through me, urging me to take a breath before I passed out. But my mind was fixated on one thought: she was gone. Just like that, poof, she had disappeared into thin air.

And I was going to burn the city down to find her.

I

DETECTIVE MATTHEW ROCKLAN

Ring Ring Ring, Ring

The high-pitched chirping of my phone jolted me from the deep, dreamless sleep I had finally succumbed to. The weight of exhaustion pulled at my limbs as I blinked blearily at the glowing screen on my nightstand. My mind groggily registered that it was only 4 am, and I couldn't help but wonder if I should have chosen a different career path. Perhaps one that didn't require me to constantly sacrifice precious hours of rest.

I grumbled into my phone as I answered the call from my boss and Alpha, Samual Williamson. "Have I caught you at a bad time, Rock?" he asked.

"Yes, Alpha," I grumbled back, still groggy from being awakened. It was always a bit of a struggle working for your Alpha.

"Sorry, Rock, but we need you down at the harbour," he said with urgency.

"What is it?" I rasp into the phone, trying to sound alert.

"We got a floater. It looks accidental. A woman on her

morning run spotted him floating near the deck," my Alpha's voice informs me.

I let out an exasperated sigh—just another day at the job.

"Give me 20; I need to shower," I grumble, dreading the case ahead.

"Damn it, damn it, damn it," I grumbled as I sat up and rubbed my hand over my face. My mouth felt gritty and dry like a sandstorm from Alice Springs had blown into it. The thought of changing careers crossed my mind once again. It seemed like I couldn't remember the last time I had a full night's sleep; this job had taken its toll on me for the past decade. At 32 years old, my body and soul aged beyond their years. Every day was a battle to keep going and pushing through the exhaustion and stress.

As a wolf shifter, one would assume that my body possessed superhuman healing abilities and quick recovery time. While that is partly true, it doesn't prevent the daily aches and pains from taking their toll. I've been shot three times in the line of duty and stabbed once - all wounds that would have killed a regular human being. But for me, they were just minor setbacks.

I thought of giving up this dangerous life and settling for a mundane job stocking shelves at Woolworths. The idea seemed more appealing each day as my body cried out for a break from the constant strain it endured. Then I remembered the thrill of the chase, the adrenaline rush of a successful mission, and I knew I could never give that up.

After 20 minutes, I had completed my morning routine: the three essential S's - Shit, Shower, and Shave. As I exited my apartment building and approached the car, I felt refreshed and ready to start the day. However, I knew that I needed sustenance in the form of food and caffeine if I wanted to be a pleasant person to be around. Luckily, I remembered the charming cafe on the deck that would surely have opened by now. The thought of a warm cup of coffee and a freshly baked pastry made my stomach growl with anticipation.

After a quick 10-minute drive, I finally reach the bustling harbour. Being a cop has its perks, one of them being able to park wherever I need and want to. City life is a mix of wonder and chaos. Every night on the job brings something new and exciting, but unfortunately, that also means never having a night off. The city never sleeps; it's alive at all hours of the day. That's why I chose to make this city my home.

Growing up in a small, uneventful town was never my cup of tea. I craved constant movement and adventure in my life; as someone who hadn't yet found their mate, my high sex drive needed to be satisfied regularly by anyone or anything that caught my fancy. But I couldn't complain - the freedom to explore without any ties or commitments was exactly what I wanted. The thought of settling down and having pups had never appealed to me, at least not yet. Maybe it would all change once I met my destined mate. There were so many conflicting accounts about what it felt like to meet them. Some claimed it was an instant, undeniable reaction, while others said it was a subtle feeling that grew over time. But one thing was for sure: you couldn't truly know until you finally knotted and marked them as your own.

My alpha's low and commanding voice cuts through the noise of the crowded harbour. I strain to catch a glimpse of him through the sea of people. He is standing on the other side of the police caution tape and talking with Miles and Henry. Determinedly pushing my way through the curious onlookers, I reach for the tape and lift it to pass through.

My Alpha turns to face me, his features drawn in concern.

"What does it look like?" I asked

Miles shrugs nonchalantly. "No distinctive signs. Might be an accident, might not, I'm guessing drunk."

"Maybe he fell over the railing," suggests Henry, gesturing towards the nearby harbour. "And was unable to swim?"

I turn to my alpha, confused. "So why was I called in?" I frown.

Samuel shook his head as we stood on the harbour, its pristine white security cameras perched high above us.

"He doesn't show up on the security cameras," he says, pointing upwards.

"So how did he get here?" I inquire, my eyes scanning the area for any clues. "The tide, perhaps?"

"Maybe," Samuel replied.

I curse under my breath. This was not going to be an easy case.

"Alright, where is the woman?" I demand, turning to face the deck.

Miles points towards a figure sitting with their back to us, engaged in conversation with Li.

"With Li," he responds.

"Has anyone taken her statement?"

"Yerp," Miles confirms. "She didn't see anything. Just the floater called it in and waited for police to arrive."

My frustration grows as I realize how little information we have to work with. The woman remains oblivious to our presence as she continues her conversation with Li. But we can't afford to waste more time - we must find out what happened here and who this mysterious floater is.

With an exasperated huff, I reluctantly agree to introduce myself and get Li to send me a copy of the statement. My tired body yearns for the comfort of my bed. It feels like I'm running on glitter and stardust. As I approach Li, conversing with a group of women, I catch a whiff of a delicious scent in the air. The blend of Lavender and Vanilla envelopes me, mingling with a mysterious earthy aroma reminiscent of wet pine bark. It's a unique, pleasant, alluring combination, pulling me closer with each step.

"Hey Li," I say, my hand clapping her on the shoulder with a friendly thud. She greets me with a warm smile that reaches up to her eyes.

"Hay Rock. This is ...."

I gaze to that delicious scent that drew me in and made my heart race. My eyes met hers, and mesmerizing moss green looked back at me.

My body began to vibrate, my wolf fighting to break free from its human shell. I felt my eyes change, yellow sparks flickering in the depths of my irises.

Shit.

Something has triggered a change within me, and I struggled to maintain control as my inner wolf claws at the surface, begging to take over.

As I turn on my heel, a low growl escapes deep within my chest. My eyes narrowed in frustration as I returned to my Alpha, determined to figure out what happened. As I approach him, I look up and lock eyes with Samuel. His brows are furrowed in concern as he asks, "What happened? Why were you triggered?"

I can feel the heat rising in my cheeks as I struggle to explain, "I don't know...I looked at the woman, and she triggered my wolf." The words escape through gritted teeth as I try to reign in my inner beast. At that moment, all I could focus on was the overpowering scent of her.

"Stop shifting," Samuel barked at me, his voice deep and commanding. Instantly, I felt the vibrations in my body come to a halt. Relief flooded me as I realized I hadn't struggled with my wolf since I was just a pup.

"Thank god," I muttered, taking a deep breath to calm myself. "Thank you, Alpha,"

"I'll deal with the woman; you go home for some rest. It's clear you needed more than I thought," Samuel stated firmly, his alpha tone leaving no room for argument. I expect to see you in the office tomorrow at 8," he added, nodding before turning around and dismissing me.

2

LILY JAMES

Was this happening? I mean, how could one person be this unlucky? One minute, I was running along the dock, enjoying the quietness of the morning when no one was around. Just for this moment in time, I could escape the memories of my past with the music pumping in my ears and the feel of my heart beating hard as I tried to beat my run time, and the next, I was sitting on this dock being interviewed by a detective.

All I wanted to do today was run off this nagging feeling that I have felt for the last few weeks, the feeling that someone is watching me everywhere I go and then I come across a body floating in the water near the dock. I want to say it's the first dead body I've seen. Wouldn't it be nice to be that sheltered, but that nice, safe life wasn't in the cards for me.

It wasn't always that way. I grew up in a happy family where I felt safe, loved and well, just like a normal girl with a normal life, but that all changed just over a year ago.

I am torn from my thoughts when I hear, "Hi Li," the deep, husky voice says as his hand claps the detective's shoulder that I have been talking to.

"Hi Rock, this is…" The Detective starts to say, but as my attention is drawn from Detective Li to the man who has just arrived, all sounds seem to go silent, and the world stills as I look up at the hottest man I have ever seen. His jaw is so sharply chiseled, his hair is a dusty brown, and his eyes, well, his eyes are like looking at the Mediterranean ocean on a stormy night; they are a dark blue with a hint of grey, and they are mesmerizing. And how he looks at me is like he can see into my soul.

As I continue to stare up into his eyes, I feel so drawn to him in a way I cannot explain, almost like I know him, but I know that cannot be the case; I haven't been in the city long, and I have tried to keep a low profile since coming here. As all these thoughts run through my head, I notice his eyes change color almost to a shade of yellow, but that can't be; it must be some reflection. When I open my mouth to say something, he beats me to it.

"I'll be right back," he almost growls at Detective Li. I wonder if I did something to offend him, or maybe he recognizes me, and I almost panic.

"Is that all you need from me?" I say, shooting to my feet as I look at the back of the other detective as he walks over to where a group of men are standing, fuck I need to get the hell out of here, I think to myself as I look back at Detective Li.

"Yes, Ms James, thank you for your time. If we need anything else, we will reach out to you on the number you provided," Detective Li says, tapping at her notebook, where she had taken down my contact number.

"Great, well, I will be going then," I say as I rush past the detective and don't look back until I get far enough away that if they began chasing me, I could get away with no issues.

Then and only then do I take a look back and, in the distance, see him look around quickly like he is searching for something, or maybe someone, and I hold my breath, but then he shakes his head and walks off in the opposite direction, and I slowly let out the breath I had been holding.

"Get a grip," I say out loud, trying to steady my racing heart.

I run back to my apartment and quickly get out my keys to enter the secured front entry; as I turn the key in the lock, I feel the hairs on the back of my neck stand up. I hurry to unlock the gate, opening it just enough to slide inside and slam it shut. When I'm safe inside the gate, I turn back towards the street and look around, searching for anyone who looks out of place. I don't see anything or anyone, but I still can not shake the feeling that someone is watching me, and my body feels it, too. My heart is racing and the hairs on my arms and neck are still standing on edge as I wrap my arms around my waist and turn to walk inside.

Once safely inside my apartment, I shower to wash off the morning. While standing under the rushing water, I close my eyes. Yellow eyes flash in my mind as I do, and I gasp, remembering the Detective.

Rock was the name that the other Detective Li had called him. I started to think about how he had looked at me, how I felt so drawn to him and how I could have sworn his eyes had changed from dark blue-grey to yellow, but how could that even be possible?

I don't know how long I stood there under the running water thinking about him, Detective Rock. Still, it must have been a while as the water began to run cold and shocked me back to reality. I quickly turned off the shower, got out and toweled off, quickly getting ready for work. Hopefully, my day will improve because, let's face it, discovering a dead body first thing in the morning wasn't fun; I mean, my day had to get better.

3

DETECTIVE MATTHEW ROCKLAN

As soon as I stepped into my apartment, I knew sleep was exactly what I needed—the day had been long and tiring, filled with endless hours of detective work and chasing down leads. Stripping back down to just my boxers, I collapsed onto my bed, grateful for the soft comfort of my mattress. My room was pitch black thanks to the heavy blackout curtains I had invested in, and the air was cool and refreshing thanks to my state-of-the-art aircon unit.

But even with these ideal sleeping conditions, my mind refused to shut off. My body felt tired, but my thoughts were still racing. Counting sheep or trying different relaxation techniques did nothing to calm my restless mind.

It seemed my wolf was as fixated on the mysterious woman from this morning as I was. Those bewitching moss-green eyes were burned into my memory, haunting me even now. I had never been so captivated by a woman, which unsettled me. To make matters worse, I hadn't been triggered by anyone in years, let alone a woman. It was a strange feeling that left me uneasy and confused simultaneously.

The jolt of adrenaline from earlier was still running through my body, overriding my exhaustion and fatigue. My muscles grew tensed, ready for action. I knew my alpha would punish me if I returned to the office now. But I couldn't just do nothing.

With a swift movement, I sat up in bed and leaped out, grabbing my laptop. I could still work from home if I couldn't work in the office. Fingers flying over the keyboard, I logged into my account and anxiously checked for any updates from Li. Perhaps she had uploaded the woman's details or her statement. It was pure curiosity driving me.

Finally finding today's file, I eagerly clicked on it and began scanning the information. Lily James, 30 years old, recently relocated to Sydney from Perth and is currently employed as a receptionist at a law firm on Elizabeth St. A photo of her from 12 years ago was attached—a mugshot. This was getting interesting.

Hesitating briefly, I clicked on her photo, and a new file appeared.

Charged with recklessly stealing a car for a joyride with her friends in Perth, she was sentenced to 6 months of good behavior and 200 hours of community service. But that was all that appeared on her file—not even a speeding ticket. It seemed like she was a rebellious teenager who had since straightened out her life. Good for her.

I continued to scroll through the rest of her file, searching for clues or evidence to help solve this case. So far, there was no footage of the body being dumped, floating in water, or falling from a height before drowning. The body was still fresh, no more than 6 hours old. How did it end up here?

It would be at least two days before we receive the fingerprint analysis. The coroner wouldn't be able to provide any information until after examining the body.

Feeling exhausted and defeated, I started to close my laptop and contemplated getting some much-needed sleep. But then I remembered the nearby tab I had left open in Safari, directing me straight to Porn Hub. With a heavy sigh, I typed "brown hair and green eyes" into the search bar - I might as well continue with today's theme.

With a finger flick, I chose the first alluring video on my screen. My eager cock strains against the fabric of my boxers as I spit on my hand and rub it over the tip, giving myself a few pulls to get the blood pumping.

But as I watch the woman on the screen doing a sultry strip tease, I realize with disappointment that she looks nothing like Lily. Cursing under my breath, I slam my laptop shut and throw it across my bed.

Closing my eyes instead, it doesn't take much for her image to flood my mind. Those moss-green eyes, so full of fire and passion, have imprinted themselves on my retinas for life. Her long brown hair was soft and silky enough to wrap around my fist as I fucked her from behind. Damn, just thinking about her was enough to make me hard.

I can almost see her now, down on her knees in front of me, palms resting on her thighs facing upwards, face turned towards the floor in submission. The thought has my inner wolf howling with desire. I know I won't last long if I keep imagining her like this.

As images of her flood my mind, I can feel my knot starting to swell - an odd sensation since it doesn't happen when I masturbate. But this woman...she's different. Something about her draws me in, something primal and wild.

I haven't knotted anyone in years, but this woman is someone I want to explore. And as I continue to fantasise about her tilted head meeting my gaze, mouthing the words "Yes, Alpha," I come undone.

My body trembles as I release my hot, sticky cum all over my stomach and chest. A primal moan escaped my lips as ecstasy washed over me. It had been so long since I had felt this kind of pleasure, and it was all because of her. The memory of her scent made this orgasm far more intense than any with the faceless women I had been with in recent years. As my breathing slowed, I climbed out of bed and headed to the shower to clean myself.

4

LILY JAMES

I arrived at work with a coffee and 5 minutes to spare. Quickly heading to the kitchen to put my lunch in the fridge, as I walked through the office, I noticed that Ryan was not at his desk and was always at his desk at this time of the day. Maybe he is sick or on holiday, and relief floods through me. Today, I won't have to try and avoid him and his flirty comments and advances. The guy wasn't bad, but he could not get the hint that I was not interested and never would be. Not just because he is my co-worker but because he isn't my type. He is no Detective Rock, I think to myself and almost slap myself for having that thought.

"Get him out of your head already," I tell myself. Hoping that way, I might listen to myself because my internal thoughts were clearly not getting the message.

I leave the kitchen and head back to the front of the office, where my desk is. When I reach my desk, I turn on my computer, sit, and go through my emails while sipping my coffee.

"Good Morning, Gorgeous," I hear my work best friend Lisa say as she enters the office.

"Good Morning, Beautiful," I answer her as I look up and see her floating through the front door.

I am not even joking. The woman is flawless, with her pin-straight, long blonde hair, not a strand out of place, and crystal blue eyes. She had legs for days, dominating in a tight black suit, pant ensemble and bright pink shirt.

"Looking amazing as always," I add, standing up and kissing her on the cheek as a greeting when she reaches my desk.

"You look tired," she says, taking in my appearance. "I mean, gorgeous outfit, but girl, you look like you haven't slept; anything you want to tell me?" she asks in a sly tone like she is hoping I will tell her I got lucky last night or something.

But no such luck; I haven't been able to go there for some time now. Trust was one issue, safety was a whole other for me, and attraction was the biggest. If I were going to put myself out there, he would have to be worth it, like Detective Rock worth it, fuck, here we go again. I curse at myself for yet again thinking about him.

"Sooo…?" Lisa presses when I don't answer tapping her fingers on my desk.

"Sorry to disappoint, but it's been a rough morning."

Lisa's demeanor changes instantly as she straightens up, and her face looks concerned as she asks, "Are you ok?"

"I can't talk about it," I answer her.

Lisa looked me up and down, and I waited for her to push me further, but she must have seen something on my face that said, "Please, not today."

She shrugs and says, "I am here if you need to talk. " She

smiles at me and reaches out to give my arm a reassuring squeeze. Lisa doesn't know fully about my past. Still, she knows enough that I have difficulty sleeping and am always on high alert everywhere I go.

"Thank you," I tell her, giving her a genuine smile for her kindness.

"Well, I am off to see what fun is installed for me today in my caseload," Lisa says waving goodbye as she strides from reception towards her office.

"Good luck," I call after her and return to work.

A few hours later, it was lunchtime, and I headed towards the break room to grab my lunch. As I entered, I saw Julia and John sitting at the table, huddled together in hushed tones. I wondered what gossip they were now spreading around the office.

"Hi, guys," I say, smiling at them as I head to the fridge.

I did not care what they were discussing, as I do not get involved in office gossip. However, I have been at the receiving end of their wagging tongues a few times, and it's never true or reliable.

"Lily," Julia says in her high-pitched voice.

I inwardly groan, wondering what wonderful stories she will tell me today. I grab my lunch and close the fridge, just hoping to get this over with.

"Did you hear…?"

"Hear what?" I ask Julia, folding my arms over my chest.

I have tried ignoring her in the past or saying I didn't want to hear, but each time, it only made things worse for me. So now I hear what she has to say and then throw it away like the grain of sand it is worth.

"Ryan didn't show up to work today, didn't even call in," John advised with a bored tone.

He does not even look in my direction; he turns the pages of his notepad, like he, too, is over the constant gossiping.

"I'm sure he will have a good explanation," I voiced to the two gossip queens, not wanting to add fuel to the fire, even though I found it strange that he didn't call to let even his boss know he wasn't coming in.

Ryan was always there when I arrived and left for the day.

"It might have been a family emergency or something?" I added, holding up my lunch to inform them I was heading to lunch. I turned on my heels and exited as fast as possible.

The rest of the day was pretty uneventful, and at 5 p.m., I packed up my desk, turned off my computer and left work for the day. I got home 30 minutes later, as the trams ran on time, and I lived close to the city center. As I entered my apartment, I sighed in relief—what a day it had been. I was tired and hungry, but I still couldn't stop thinking about today, mainly one thing: Detective Rock.

Considering I saw a dead body this morning, my thoughts were only ever drawn back to the handsome detective, which was saying a lot. I was completely drawn to him and I didn't know why, so drawn in fact that I grabbed my laptop and started to google him. A bunch of Google results came up, but nothing with Detective Rock, so I added Sydney, Australia, and a result about Detective Matthew Rocklan appeared. I scrolled through the pages until I found a picture, and I immediately knew this was my Detective Rock.

There weren't many pictures of him for me to ogle at, but who was I kidding? I didn't need pictures to remember his appearance; his face and body were etched like I had stared at him daily for a year. After reading through some articles, I sensed that Detective Matthew Rocklan lived for the job and not much else, so I decided to close my laptop and get dinner.

"Matt," I said out loud to myself.

"I like it," I added as I walked to the kitchen.

Eating dinner alone sucked some nights, and tonight was one of those nights; I craved to know what it would be like to come home to someone every night, to cook for someone and have them cook for you.

Instead, it was a quick meal of salmon, rice and veggies. It was boring, but it was good for me. I was trying to improve my eating habits, eating clean and healthy, at least during the week.

I started this new habit after I called my local Chinese last week. Instead of placing an order, they said, 'Usual order?' When I called, they said, 'Usual order?' When the delivery girl delivered my order, she said, 'Same time, same order next week,' and left. That is when I knew I had become that lady—the predictable, lonely lady. All I needed was a bunch of cats, and I would be complete.

LATER THAT NIGHT, I CRAWLED INTO BED, EXHAUSTED FROM the day—so much so that I didn't even take my extra pillows off the bed; I just crawled around them. It was so nice and cozy, all secure in the blankets and pillows, almost as a security wall around me. I fell asleep almost instantly.

Blue eyes with shades of grey looked into my eyes as if he were looking into my soul. He wrapped his arms around me, pulling me close to his body. It was like I had never felt so safe and never wanted that feeling to disappear. I cuddled into him, resting my head against his chest. I just wanted to be closer to him; after a few minutes, Matt put his hand under my chin and slowly tilted my head back to look up into his beautiful, mesmerizing eyes. Without saying a word, he crashed his lips onto mine, and we began to devour each other, tasting each other, exploring each other's mouths with our tongues and bodies with our hands. It was like a frenzy of sorts, both of us unable to get enough of the other person. I wanted more; I wanted everything from him; I ached for him; I needed him.

Matt started to lift my tank top, first exposing my stomach and then my bra. I pulled away from our kiss long enough to lift my arms in the air so that he could remove the tank completely; I followed suit and began to unbutton his light blue shirt starring up at him as I bit my lip. He growls like growls, and it's the hottest thing I have ever heard come out of a man. I undo the last button and pull his shirt off his shoulders, and it falls to the ground, pooling at his feet. This man is a god; he looks like he has been chiseled from stone by a master craftsman; he is perfect and toned. I run my hands over his abs while I stare up into his eyes, and He doesn't take his eyes off me either; the moment is so intense; we are just two people looking into each other's souls, and I didn't want the moment to end. Still, I did want to feel his hands on me like I had my hands on him.

I take a step forward and press my body up against his, and he takes the hint; he pulls me against his body and then, with one arm locked around my back, his other hand begins to move up the side of my body, cupping my breast still in my bra. Then he continues up to my shoulders and behind my neck. He pulls me into him just a little closer and then kisses me again, this time more intense and possessive. I love every second of it as I possessively grip his hair, trying to get closer to him as if it was even possible.

Ring ring, ring ring, a phone began to ring, causing us to break apart with a grunt of annoyance.

Matt pulls his phone out and answers it, but the ringing doesn't stop. So I look around for my phone and see it on the nightstand. I pick it up, but my phone isn't ringing either. I look at Matt, confused, but he slowly disappears, and the annoying ringing doesn't stop.

I blink, open my eyes again, and find myself surrounded by pillows and blankets in my bed. It's then that I realize it was all just a dream. All I want to do is sleep, but my phone still rings.

I look over to my bedside table and see it light up again. I lean over and pick it up. It's only 5 a.m., and it's a private number. I am hesitant to answer it, but given that the police may be calling me, I answer.

"Hello," I say into the phone in my half-asleep voice, there is no answer on the other end, just silence.

"Hello?" I asked again if they had heard me, but there was no reply, so I quickly hung up.

I am slightly annoyed that I bothered to answer the call in the first place because it woke me up from that amazing dream. I throw my phone down on the edge of the bed and roll over on my bed, pulling the blankets over my head with a huff. I try my hardest to go back to sleep, but now that I am awake, I have no chance, so I decided to get up and go for my morning run instead.

5

As the soft light of the receding moon was filtering through my bedroom window, I stirred from my slumber. Excitement bubbled in my chest as I remembered my plans for a morning run before the city woke up. Living in the bustling metropolis had its perks. Still, it also had its downsides - like being unable to shift and run freely within city limits. So, I quickly changed into snug sweatpants and sneakers and headed out of my apartment.

Stepping out onto the deserted streets, I approached the city's outskirts. It was a 40-minute drive to reach one of my favorite spots—a national park amidst rolling hills and dense forests. As I drove, the buildings and bright lights gradually gave way to open spaces and quiet tranquility.

Despite popular belief, the city did have its moments of peaceful stillness. Like now, when the streets were empty, no one was around except for a few nocturnal animals scurrying about. The hum of traffic and noise pollution faded, replaced by the gentle rustling of leaves and birdsong.

Reaching the park's entrance, I parked my car and entered

the cool morning air. A sense of calm washed over me as I took in the lush greenery surrounding me. This was my sanctuary, my escape from the chaos of city life.

I move deeper into the dense thicket, weaving through towering trees and gnarled roots that threaten to trip me. Carefully, I shed my clothes and conceal them under a thick brush, feeling a familiar tingle race down my spine. Shifting is not a painless process. As my body transforms from human to wolf, every bone seems to shatter and realign. It's an excruciating but necessary ordeal.

Before long, my surroundings transform into a vivid blur of sights, sounds, and scents. My ears perk up to the symphony of rustling leaves and chirping birds while my nose picks up on the intricate scents of the forest - damp earth, pine needles, and the faint trace of prey. My eyes adjust to bring in a world painted in different hues and sharper focus. Unlike popular belief, wolves can see in color - though the shades are slightly muted compared to our human form.

With a burst of energy, I take off on my usual route, leaping easily over fallen trees and splashing through the small river that winds through the woods. The freedom of running in my shifted form brings back memories of being a playful pup - carefree and full of mischief. A pang of loneliness hits as I realize I have no one to run with unless the entire pack or an organized run is planned. For safety reasons, we avoid drawing attention by running alone or in small groups when necessary. After all, a large group of wolves roaming freely in Australian parks would surely raise some eyebrows.

As the sun began to crest over the horizon, I looked up and realized I needed to return to my clothes quickly. Shifting back into my human form, I hurriedly dressed before anyone could spot me. Though I was in a National Park, parading around naked at any hour would surely raise some unwanted questions if I were caught.

Jumping into my car, I noticed a few missed calls from my Alpha. It was only 4:30 am; what could he possibly want? I had planned to be in the office at 8.

With a sense of urgency, I dialed Samuel back.

"Matt," he answered.

"Morning, Alpha," I replied.

"We have another body," he informed me.

"Same MO as the last?" I asked.

"No, this one was found in a parking lot on Elizabeth Street."

"I'm out at Heathcote National Park, but I'll head home and get changed," I said.

"I've already called Liam and Luke. They'll be here in 10 minutes, so hurry up," he instructed before hanging up the phone.

"Yes, Alpha," I mumbled, knowing he couldn't hear me. My mind raced with thoughts of the murder and how it connected to our killer.

The streets are becoming increasingly congested with traffic, and I know that by the time I reach my apartment, I will be quicker to leap over the buses than to drive through the crowded roads down to Elizabeth. Hurriedly showering, I wear a pair of sleek black slacks and a simple button-up shirt. I don't like wearing a suit daily, but I bend the rules slightly with my attire. I have no sense of cold like most humans; wolves run hot naturally, so wearing a heavy jacket in any weather suffocates me. Instead, I opt for the thinnest black slacks I can find; the more expensive and tailored, the heavier and thicker the material.

Rushing out of my apartment, I deftly jump onto the closest bus on my closest route and disembark onto George Street. The walk up to Elizabeth will do wonders for my legs after my morning run, a testament to my physical strength.

As I reach the parking lot, I notice that the entire underground area is cordoned off with tape, leaving no way in or out. We will surely have some irate commuters this morning, but thankfully, Li is skilled at handling difficult situations. I am leaning towards being less sociable myself.

I walk past the barricade and nod to the uniformed patrolman operating it before continuing down the ramp quickly.

My heart races as I see Liam and Luke huddled together, deep in conversation with Sam. I waste no time joining them and blur out my question: "What do we have?"

Luke responds quickly, his voice grave and professional. "Female victim, brown hair, green eyes. It appears to be a mugging, but something doesn't add up. She's dressed in running gear and still has her phone and keys on her."

My pulse quickens as I catch sight of the body they're discussing. Between two parked cars lies a woman in bright pink running clothes, her medium-length brown hair matted against her face. Two stab wounds mar her abdomen, and hand prints are visible around her neck.

"Is it the witness from yesterday?" I ask frantically, fear creeping into my voice.

Liam shakes his head from behind me. "No, she looks different. But we should check on her well-being."

I volunteered immediately, knowing my wolf wouldn't let me rest until I did so.

"I'll do it," I declare, pointing at Liam, who smirks back at me.

"Of course, Rock," he teases.

As we wait for the coroner to arrive, Liam informs us that forensics is almost done with the scene and the body will soon be bagged and tagged. He also mentions how this incident may appease some of the angry workers who have been complaining about parking issues.

"Do we have any witnesses?" I inquire.

Luke answers quickly, "None at all."

Sam chimes in then, adding: "The security guard found her when he arrived for work at 4 am. He does his rounds every morning."

I furrow my brow at this new piece of information. "But why would someone be out running at that hour in the city?"

Liam shrugs, a sly smile playing on his lips. "Well, except for us."

The woman was clad in form-fitting shorts and a cropped tank top. She would have surely been cold in that outfit. I couldn't help but raise an eyebrow in disbelief. Who goes for a run at that hour? But then again, I can't judge, considering I was also out and about. As I shrugged nonchalantly, the coroner approached us from around the corner of the car.

"I hope you boys haven't touched her," he deadpans with annoyance.

I held up my hands defensively. "Nope, I kept all my fingers and toes to myself," I quipped back with a smirk.

Liam chimes in with a mischievous grin. "I just got here; I haven't had the chance to piss you off yet."

The coroner shakes his head before crouching down near the girl's body. His movements are careful and precise as he examines her lifeless form.

"Come on, Rock, let's get some coffee and head to the office," Liam suggests, breaking me out of my thoughts.

Coffee sounded like a good idea right now. Maybe we could swing by that welfare check afterward.

6

It is just after 10 a.m. when I look up from my desk, and for a minute, I think I am having another dream because walking towards the front of my office, it was him, Detective Matthew Rocklan, with another man.

My heart starts to pound as he opens the door and strides into the office, his eyes meeting mine as soon as he enters. I stand up to greet him, feeling too small in their presence to stay seated.

They both wear suit pants, and their legs show that they work out regularly, and leg day is never missed. I can see they are built and toned in all areas, the muscles in their shirts showing as the material clings to their bodies with every movement.

"Ms James," he says as he reaches my desk, "Detective Rocklan, we met briefly yesterday morning."

He reached out a hand for me to shake. He leans his body against the front of my desk, blocking it from my view, which is very annoying as I was enjoying looking at it. "Oh my god, stop it," I inwardly curse at myself.

I give myself a mental slap to pull myself together, 'Do not embarrass yourself in front of this man,' I tell myself.

"I remember good morning, Detective Rocklan," I answer while taking his hand and shaking it.

Our hands linger a little longer than in a typical handshake. I feel like I can't let him go like I need to touch him.

He doesn't pull away, either, and we stare at each other in silence, just holding hands and getting lost in the moment, the whole world around us melting away.

"Ah-hm," the man with Matt clears his throat.

We both drop our hands as we come out of our trance, and my attention is drawn to the man with Matt. I can feel that my cheeks are heated, and I know they both can see it, but I wasn't the only one in that moment, so I can't be completely embarrassed by it, not all on my own at least.

Frowning, I notice that Matt doesn't seem phased, and the other man doesn't show any sign that he sees my embarrassment, so I move on.

"Sorry," I say, "was there something else you needed for my statement,"

"We are just here to conduct a welfare check," the other man states.

I assume he is a detective, as he looks like one of the men I saw with Matt yesterday at the dock.

"Welfare check?" I ask, "For Ryan? He still isn't in today, I am afraid. " I look to the main office toward Ryan's desk and then back to the men before me.

"Ryan?" Detective Rocklan questions with a raised brow, looking at the other man with a questioning look.

"Yes, Ryan, my co-worker. He hasn't been heard of the last

few days and didn't even call the office to let anyone know he wouldn't be here," I state.

"It is completely out of character for him; he lives for this job," I advise the two men. I'm starting to wonder why two detectives have been put on the case. It seems odd unless they know why Ryan is missing, or maybe he isn't missing anymore, and dread rolls over me.

"We don't know anything about Ryan?" Matt frowns.

"Detective Henry and I were doing a welfare check on you," Matt says, looking at me.

"But you say that your co-worker Ryan is missing?" he asks me.

"Yes, he didn't show up yesterday or today to work," I state.

It dawns on me that he said they were doing a welfare check on me.

"Why would you be doing a welfare check on me?" I ask with furrowed brows. "I was just the one that found the body; I didn't see anyone. From what I heard, the body had been in the water for hours, so I didn't even get close to seeing anyone dump the body?" I question.

"The body of a female matching your description was found this morning," Detective Henry advised me.

Shocked to my core, I look at Henry and Rocklan, my eyes pin-ponging between the two.

"Oh my, that's horrible," I state, startled by the revelation.

My hand automatically goes to my mouth in horror and shock; thoughts begin to run through my head so fast.

Are the cases related?

"Am I in danger?" I ask before I can stop myself.

Fear creeping in. Fear that I haven't felt this intense for

months now but still familiar enough that I feel a tightening in my chest as my breathing gets shallow and intense.

"We aren't sure if the cases are related, but we do not believe you are in immediate danger," Matt began, placing a comforting hand over mine.

The touch is brief but enough to calm me, and then he takes it back and steps away from the desk.

"Like you told Detective Li, you didn't see anyone dump the body; you merely found it, so we don't suspect anyone is after you," he adds as he watches my reaction as if searching for something.

I watch his hand fists by his side like he is trying to control himself or is angry at the situation, which makes me curious why he is reacting this way.

Was he lying? Am I in danger, or was he frustrated because he didn't know the answer but wanted to reassure me as best he could?

"Right, I didn't see anything at all in that nature, just some-thing floating in the water and when I went to get a closer look, I saw the body and called the police right away," I recon-firmed to Matt and Detective Henry what I had already informed Detective Li of.

Again, Matt eyed me like he was searching for something in me or wanting to see if I was being honest or hiding something.

Normally, with this sort of intensity, I would call it out or shy away for it to stop. But I liked his intensity and wanted him to look at me, to know me, to know I would never do anything like that, that I would never lie to him, not about something like this.

Whatever he saw in my reaction must have shown him I

was telling the truth because he nodded before shifting his gaze over my body and back up to my eyes. For a split second, I could have sworn I had seen those yellow eyes again, the ones from yesterday, the ones I had seen before he had excused himself.

Then they are gone again, and I notice Detective Henry stiffen next to Matt. It is only for a second, but it is enough to draw my attention in his direction and away from Matt.

"Thank you for your time, Ms James," Detective Henry began. We will be in touch if we need anything else. Please don't hesitate to call if you think of anything else."

I didn't want Matt to leave. I racked my brain trying to think of something to say, but everything that came to mind made me sound like a stalker or pathetic.

So I remained silent and let them leave, watching as they walked through the glass doors and into the elevator. Both turned around as the doors to the elevator closed, with Matt looking straight at me and Detective Henry moving into his line of sight, pulling Matt's gaze away from me.

My heart was racing; what was that? What had made me so attracted to this man?

Sure, he was hot, but so was Detective Henry. But with Matt, it was something else. I was drawn to him as I needed him, and I couldn't shake the feeling that I would see him again, and I hoped it would be soon.

7

DETECTIVE MATTHEW ROCKLAN

My wolf was captivated by this girl. Every time I took a breath, her alluring scent filled my nostrils, and my wolf would wag its tail excitedly. I had never experienced such a strong pull towards someone before. Could she be my destined 'mate'? The only way to know for sure was to mate with her. The mere thought of it caused my erection to stir in my pants. I needed to regain control of my mind and body.

"Are you alright, Rock?" Henry asked, noticing my strange behavior.

"I'm fine, just feeling a bit off whenever I see that woman," I replied, shaking my head.

"I've noticed, too. You act differently around her. I swear, I've seen your eyes change a few times," Henry raised his eyebrows at me.

"Honestly, my wolf desires her. Every time I catch her scent, he longs to come out and play," I growled in frustration. "It's inconvenient and annoying."

"Well, give him what he wants," Henry chuckled at me.

The elevator dinged as the doors opened on the ground floor.

"That noise is deafening!" Henry cursed at the elevator. "Why can't they make them silent?"

"They have a nose for blind people, you idiot! So they know when it's time to get off," I laughed at him.

"As if they don't hear the loud screech of the doors sliding open," Henry retorted.

"Stop being a shit cunt" I laugh at him. "We got two murders to solve now."

As I stepped out of the building and onto the bustling street, my ears were instantly assaulted by the chaotic symphony of city noise. The screeching of car horns, blaring music from passing cars, and the constant chatter of people rushing to their destinations filled the air. The pungent scent of human bodies mingled with various odors - some pleasant, some not so much. As I returned to my car, I caught whiffs of unwashed individuals and others who had indulged in quick trysts before starting their day. I couldn't help but smirk at the latter, knowing that their attempts at hiding it with neatly combed hair and pressed suits were in vain.

Finally settling into the passenger seat of my cruiser, I pulled out my phone and dialed Miles' number. "Hey, Rock," he answered on the second ring.

"Can you contact the coroner for me? I need to see if we can expedite the floater case," I said urgently.

"Any particular reason?" Miles asked curiously.

"A missing person from Ms James's workplace hasn't shown up for days. My gut tells me they might be the same," I explained, trusting my intuition.

"I'll make the call now, but no promises. He just picked up a fresh case this morning," Miles replied with amusement.

"Just do your best to sweet-talk him into it," I chuckled, knowing Miles' smooth-talking skills too well.

"Will do. Are you guys heading into the office now?" he asked.

"Yes, we're on our way there now," I confirmed.

"I'm assuming you found Ms James to be fit and healthy?" Miles' response was laced with a smile, his words carrying the sound of it to my ear.

"We didn't just find her fit and healthy," Henry chimed in from the driver's seat, his voice betraying amusement. My wolf growled low within me at his words.

"Ohhh looks like Rock has caught the love bug!" Miles teased, his laughter echoing through the car.

I glared at Henry, who sat there trying (and failing) to contain his laughter. That bastard knew exactly how I would react to that comment.

"Shut up," I grunted, ending the call and shoving my phone back into my pocket. "My wolf just...reacts to her."

"Sure he does," Henry chuckled as he pulled into our office parking lot.

"Drop me off on the street," I ordered, craving coffee to calm my nerves.

As we pulled into our building's underground parking lot, I hopped out of the car and headed straight for the coffee shop on the ground floor. Pushing open the door and stepping inside, I immediately spotted Katie behind the counter.

"Hey Katie, can I get the usual and a toastie?" I requested when I reached the counter.

"Of course, Rock," she smiled warmly at me.

I stepped aside and waited for my order, my mind racing over everything that had happened this morning. The image of that runner looking eerily similar to Lily filled me with worry. Was someone intentionally targeting women who looked like her? Or was it just a strange coincidence? I never believed in coincidences, especially not in my line of work.

"Here you are, Rock," Katie's long, slender fingers hand me my toastie and coffee, brushing against mine with a subtle touch that sends tingles up my arm. Her mischievous wink only adds to the electric charge between us.

We had a fling about six months ago. Still, Katie didn't seem to understand my one-and-done rule and has continued flirting with me at every opportunity. I didn't mind the attention, keeping the door open for a potential repeat encounter. But today, her touch made me feel uncomfortable and slightly disgusted, causing the hairs on my arms to stand on end.

I quickly thank her and exit, feeling my inner wolf stirring again. What was happening to me? My wolf had never caused me issues before, so why was it suddenly becoming restless now?

In a rush, I step into the elevator and press the button for the 3rd floor, anxiously waiting for the doors to close behind me.

8

LILY JAMES

Today has been moving so slowly; ever since Matt and Detective Henry were here, I have had this sinking feeling that something is wrong. It is a feeling that has lingered for a while, but it is stronger today than ever. My mind keeps going back to yesterday and the floating body and then Ryan still missing, and now a woman found this morning. The world around me was turning to shit just like it did just over a year ago, but it couldn't be the same, could it? Could I be this unlucky to have my life turned upside down again?

"No, it's just a coincidence," I told myself and laughed because I don't believe in coincidence.

People tell themselves this when they don't want to see what is staring them right in the face. God was the truth, staring me in the face, and I couldn't believe it. I prayed to every God out there that this would not happen again.

"Lily, are you okay?" a familiar voice said, breaking me from my thoughts. I looked up to find Lisa standing beside me, looking at me with concern.

"What? Sorry, I was in another world," I answered, shaking my head and smiling at her.

Lisa smiled back at me. "Hey, I've never noticed that scar before," Lisa said, staring at my arm. When I looked down at it, I realized that subconsciously, I had been rubbing at an old scar on the inside of my arm, one of many that reminded me of a past I would rather forget.

"Oh yeah, it was just a silly accident when I was a kid," I said, laughing it off.

I pulled my sleeve back over the scar. "I'm sorry. Did you need something from me?" I asked Lisa, changing the subject.

"I was wondering if you wanted to grab lunch today? I don't have any clients till 3 pm, and I could do with a yum cha lunch; it's been forever since we went out to lunch together, and I know yum cha is your favorite," Lisa said, smiling down at me with a look I recognized, Lisa wanted something. I wasn't sure what it was, but I needed something to take my mind off everything I was going through. Regardless of what she wanted from me, she was my friend, so I knew it wouldn't be horrible.

"Sure, I'd love to," I agreed, and Lisa's face lit up

"Perfect, grab your things and let's go," Lisa stated, picking up her bag from the side of my desk. I hadn't even noticed that she had it with her, but I guess I was distracted when she approached my desk.

I leaned over to the filing cabinet, opened the drawer, pulled out my handbag, pulled the strap over my shoulder and stood up. I quickly diverted the phones to the main switch, which handled all calls in the building when required and locked my computer before facing Lisa.

"Ready," I advised her.

"Yum cha, here we come," Lisa cheered, taking my arm as we walked to the glass door and towards the elevators. It was a quick walk down a few blocks to our favorite yum cha in the QVB building. The staff was great, and the food was always amazing, so we came here whenever we needed a yum cha fix. We were seated quickly, and food began to be presented to us on the carts that came around. We selected a few things to start with.

"So?" Lisa began as I chewed my first mouth-full

"Here we go," I stated, rolling my eyes

"What?" Lisa said, acting shocked

"I knew there was more to this lunch invite; you get this look," I advised her.

"What look?" Lisa asked with furrowed brows.

"I will never tell you because then you won't do the look, and I won't know that you're up to something more than you're saying," I advised her, laughing as Lisa put on her Sookie face, the one she always turned on when she wanted to know something but someone wasn't giving into her.

Lisa was silent for a while; she always tried to make it so awkward that people just gave in and told her, but I wasn't falling for that.

"Get on with it. What do you want from me?" I said, gesturing for her to continue and tell me.

"Fine," Lisa said with a huff, "Well, you know how I have been dating Josh for a few months now, and I have started to meet his family and some of his friends and…"

"No," I cut Lisa off, knowing exactly where she was headed with this conversation.

"You didn't even let me finish!" Lisa stated in an annoyed tone, the frustration written all over her face

"You don't need to finish; I know what you were going to say," I said, taking a bite of a dim sim as I pointed at her with my chopstick.

"It's time to get back on the horse," Lisa said, pointing her chopstick back at me. You haven't dated anyone the entire time I have known you, and you need to meet someone and have some fun."

She wasn't wrong. I hadn't dated anyone in a long time, not since, well… just not in a long time. I want someone to have fun with, but the only person my brain ever wanted to think about or even consider having fun with these days was Detective Rocklan.

I could not get him off my mind, and I knew that no one else would measure up to the perfect man I had built in my mind, Matt. I didn't even know the guy, but I felt he was great, and nothing seemed to change my mind.

"Well, I am right?" Lisa said, looking at me with a raised brow, which meant I had zoned out again and missed some of what she had said

"Yes, you're right. I haven't dated in a long time, but honestly, I don't think I want to," I told Lisa. The look of mortification on her face, like I had told her that I hated babies or something, made me almost laugh.

"You're not normal at all," Lisa stated.

That statement did make me laugh, "I never said I was normal," I told Lisa still laughing.

"Stop you, weirdo. You kill me, honestly," Lisa told me, shaking her head. She also began to laugh; after a few seconds, though, she got this serious look in her eyes, and her face softened.

"You never talk about what happened to you," Lisa said

quietly. My body instantly stiffened, and a cold shiver ran up my spine.

"But it's clear that something did happen to you," Lisa continued, taking my hand and holding it in hers and pulling me slightly towards her, "I know that whatever it was, it was really bad, so bad that you can't seem to let anyone in to share your life. But one day, I hope you meet someone who can break through those walls and show you that some guys out there can be trusted,"

I was suddenly overcome with emotion, and a tear ran down my cheek, not just because of my friend's beautiful words but because I prayed she was right.

"I adore you," I finally said to Lisa as she hugged me, and tears continued flowing down my cheeks.

9

DETECTIVE MATTHEW ROCKLAN

The tension in the air was palpable as I waited for a call from the coroner. It had been over two hours, and I could imagine Miles somehow managing to anger the man. Those two were like oil and water, constantly at each other's throats and pushing each other's buttons. Miles always blamed his wolf, claiming it would become agitated and restless whenever he was around our coroner colleague. But deep down, I knew Miles didn't like the man.

The entire department seemed to have a mutual dislike for him, but we all managed to maintain a professional facade. It was no secret that the man carried the heavy scent of death everywhere, which was understandable considering his line of work. But for us wolves with heightened senses, it was downright putrid.

Finally, around 4 pm, I received the long-awaited call. The body had been identified as Ryan Smalls; God dammit, it was her co-worker. Cursing under my breath, I slammed the phone down in frustration.

Jumping up from my seat, I quickly grabbed my phone and

gun holder before strapping them on. "Miles, Henry. Chief's office. Now!" My growled command echoed through the precinct.

I watch as if they are meerkats. Two heads pop up from behind their desk walls and peer at me.

Henry furrows his brow in confusion, while Miles appears slightly pale, likely anticipating trouble for something.

Boldly striding into the Alpha's office without knocking, I sit in the chair directly in front of his desk.

"What can I do for you, Rock?" Sam inquires.

I raise one finger in a gesture of needing a moment as Miles and Henry enter and position themselves behind me.

"Close the door," I command, and one of them swiftly obeys before resuming their place behind me.

"The floater has been identified as Ryan Smalls," I announce with a heavy sigh.

"Fuck," Miles and Henry exclaim in unison.

"Who is Ryan Smalls?" Sam queries, his expression filled with bewilderment.

"After finding this morning's body resembling Ms James so closely," I explain wearily, "we conducted a welfare check on her."

"Why are you smirking, Henry?" Sam directs his question at him.

"Well, it turns out Rock's wolf has quite the liking for Ms James," Henry reveals with a smug grin.

Sam's eyes fixate on me. "You know you cannot pursue that woman, Rock. She's a witness," he growls at me sternly.

"Yes, I am aware," I reply, turning my chair to face Henry, who sold me out.

"I can't control what my wolf desires. It's a new sensation

for me," I admit with a heavy sigh. "But I have it under control."

"Well, you better keep it that way. Find someone else to satisfy your urges, Rock. We can't have you sniffing around her skirts," Sam orders firmly.

I emit a low and guttural growl at the mere thought of touching another woman. What the hell is wrong with me?

Sam's piercing gaze locks onto mine, his eyebrows raising at the low rumble emanating from my throat.

"Perhaps your wolf isn't the only one drawn to her," he suggests.

"Can we please change the subject?" I snap.

"Sure, sure," our Alpha chuckles. "Continue with your report."

"As I was saying," I say through gritted teeth, flipping off whoever is snickering behind me, "we conducted a welfare check. Ms James revealed that Ryan hadn't shown up for work in days and had made no contact with the office."

"So no one knew of his whereabouts?" Sam inquires.

"Nope," I replied with a crisp 'p.' So I requested the coroner run the John Do's prints against Mr. Smalls, and they were a match."

"Let me guess," Sam says, reciting the facts. "Mr Smalls turns up as a floater in the same area where Ms James jogs daily, and now a woman fitting her description is found dead in an underground parking lot?"

"I'm starting to see too many coincidences here," I sigh.

"Have you looked into Ms James' background? Any skeletons in her closet?" Sam asks.

"Not a single one," Miles interjects. "I ran a thorough background check, and all that came up was a minor incident of joyriding in Perth when she was 18. She turned her life around after that and has stayed out of trouble ever since."

"She moved here from Perth not too long ago," Henry adds.

"So what you're saying is there's nothing noteworthy about this girl?" Sam prompts.

My frustration boils over, causing me to snarl louder than before.

Sam's deep Alpha commanding voice snaps at me, "Watch it Rock."

"This woman does something to you, mate!" Henry chimes in, his voice full of amusement.

"She isn't your mate, is she?" Miles asks, his eyes wide with awe.

"No, I don't think so," I reply calmly, trying to shake off my strange pull towards her.

"I'm starting to think there is something to that comment," Sam remarks, looking directly at me. "We might need to take you off the case, Rock. We can't have you wolfing out if anything happens."

"No! I'll be fine. I need to figure out what's going on," I insist stubbornly.

"If it comes out that she is your mate, we will have to take you off the case. It's too dangerous to have you near her when you are unbonded," Sam huffs with concern.

"Trust you to find your mate on the job," Miles laughs at me, nudging my shoulder playfully.

"Shut up, she isn't my mate," I grumble under my breath, feeling a mix of frustration and confusion.

"We shall see," Miles chuckles. "I have never seen your wolf out as much as it has in the past 10 minutes."

"Whatever. Let's focus on the case," I snap at them both, trying to regain control of my emotions and thoughts.

"Okay, okay, enough bickering. What are your plans now?" Sam interjects, taking charge of the situation once again.

"We need to go back to the harbour and figure out how the body got there at that specific time and with no footage on the cameras," I explain.

"Are there any divers available to help us investigate?" Henry asks, ever the practical one.

"I'll call and see, but it's unlikely we can get any until tomorrow," Sam states.

"We could head down to the pier and see if we can spot anything on foot. Tomorrow, we'll bring a dummy with us and have some divers take a closer look underwater," Henry suggests, always thinking ahead.

"Do we have any leads on the time of death or cause?" Sam inquires, his voice laced with frustration.

"No, all the coroner could determine was that he drowned, and it had to have happened that morning. We only have a 6-hour window for the body dump," I shrug.

"Well, that's just fantastic," Miles snarls.

"It takes time to get the full report back. We're lucky he ran the prints for us," I huff.

"Why did Mr Smalls' prints appear in the system anyway?" Henry asks.

"Ironically, a DUI 4 years ago. He blew just over the limit and got booked for it," I explain.

"That turned out to be fortunate for us," Henry remarks darkly. "But not so much for him."

I sigh and push myself up from my chair. "Let's go check out the tide and where the body was found. Maybe there's some evidence we can use."

"All right, let's go; I wanna see what's going on with this tide and placement," I huff and stand from my seat.

"Let's go, pups," I demand and leave the office.

IO

LILY JAMES

It is after 7 pm when I finally get off the tram at my stop and start walking towards my apartment. The streets are still bustling with people, with couples walking hand in hand towards local restaurants for dinner or home from an evening stroll, and it makes me think about what Lisa said today.

All these people had found someone they trusted enough to let them share their lives. Why couldn't I? Well, I knew why, but was it time to move on, get past my demons and trust someone again? I sighed, already feeling sorry for the poor man who had to try and break down my walls, they had their work cut out for them.

Then my thoughts drifted back to the one man I could not stop thinking about, Detective Rocklan.

I felt a smile creep across my face when his image appeared in my mind.

His beautiful eyes and how they looked at me like they could see into my soul; I had never been drawn so much to a man like this.

I didn't know him; I had only seen him a few times and

spoken to him once, but it felt like he saw me. Not just the fact that I was pretty but like he could see my darkness and it didn't scare him off.

It's like he knew there was more to me than what meets the eye, or maybe that is what I see in him, and I am projecting that he sees it in me, too.

As I get to my front security gate, I stop and pull out my keys when I am suddenly pushed into the gate and held there under the weight of someone. I scream at the top of my lungs, fear racing through me as I struggle to breathe, and my heart is pounding out of my chest. I can smell him, he smells of coffee, cologne and sweat and all of a sudden, the weight is off me, and someone is talking to me.

"Are you ok?" He asks

I can't really hear clearly over the raging panic going through me but as I turn a guy stands in front of me.

"I'm so sorry," he says, "Are you ok?" he adds, holding his hands up

"I didn't mean to scare you; I tripped and fell into you," he continues when I don't reply.

He looks at me with concern as I try to regain my breath. I look him up and down and note that he is wearing workout gear and runners; he has his Apple watch set to work out and is 28 minutes into his run.

I raise my hand to my chest and rub it, trying to calm my racing heart, noting that he was no danger to me and had done as he said and tripped into me.

"I'm so sorry," he states again, looking at me up and down but not in a creepy way, more like looking for injuries or a reason why I am not responding to him.

"I'm okay," I finally get out, but really I am not okay.

After years of taking self-defense classes, I let the fear immediately take over; if this guy wanted to hurt me, he could have because I didn't even try to fight back.

But then I didn't have the chance, and I was pinned under his body weight. But I knew how to get out from under someone. I had learned the techniques to calm myself in a situation like this, and I had failed; I had forgotten it all and frozen in fear.

"Are you sure you're okay?" he asks, not moving from his spot, his hands still out as if to show me he is of no harm to me.

"Yes, thank you, I am fine," I tell him, finally able to breathe again as I stand up a little taller.

I push my shoulders back to try to convince this man that I am fine and that he can go on his merry way.

"Ok," he says, taking one last look at me. I really am sorry," he says as I nod and wave him off as if permitting him to leave.

He takes this as his out and turns to leave, continuing his run down the street and into the nearby park.

After he is gone, I take a deep breath, shake my head, and head back towards the security gate. When I look down at my hands to see my keys, I notice for the first time that I have my main security key. I am holding it in my hand like I am holding a knife like I could use it as a weapon, and it occurs to me that in some deep down part of my subconscious, I hadn't just succumbed to the fear. I had prepared to defend myself when I got the chance.

My guess is that is why the guy never approached me and held his hands out the way he did, to prove to me that he was harmless because I looked like a crazy lady about to stab him with my keys.

I might have looked crazy, but I didn't care. I was glad I hadn't completely frozen, but I needed more training. I needed to learn ways to control my fear so that if something like that happened, I wouldn't let the panic take over; I would react immediately and protect myself.

When I finally made it into my apartment, I called John.

"Lily James, what can I do for you, beautiful lady," John answered on the 3rd ring.

"Hi John, I need your help," I greeted him answering his question

"I'm glad to hear you're finally ready," John said

"I am John, I am," I told him, knowing I was finally ready.

I told John what had happened and explained that I had frozen but what I had done with the keys.

He praised me for not letting fear completely rule me but agreed that I needed to reel in the fear now that I was ready to confront it head-on.

He booked me in for my first appointment tomorrow after work, and I already felt some relief; I was both looking forward to and dreading tomorrow as I knew I was going to have to deal with the demons that I was not ready to deal with the first time I trained with John, but it was time.

I was tired of always being scared and looking over my shoulder. I needed to know that I could 100% defend myself if I needed to; I needed to know that things like what happened today would never happen again.

"You can do this," I told myself as I blew out a big breath, "It's time," I added, closing my eyes and taking another deep breath, trying to center myself.

Tomorrow was a new day, and it was the start of me taking back my life in all aspects; I knew I was ready this time.

II

DETECTIVE MATTHEW ROCKLAN

Navigating the waters of Sydney Harbour was no easy feat. The tides were easily accessible through a simple Google search, but determining the floating zones proved challenging. With boats constantly coming and going, the direction of the tide would shift and change as they passed, creating a chaotic pattern that needed to be accounted for at all times.

To solve this puzzle, we planned to deploy six dummies in various locations throughout the harbor, out of view of our cameras. This would allow us to track their movement. However, this plan relied heavily on our divers, who must swim alongside the dummies and act as human substitutes when necessary.

As someone who had been on this job for years, I knew better than to expect anything to go according to plan. Something unexpected would inevitably arise when I thought I had everything figured out. It was a constant game of thinking on my feet.

"Sam just texted," Miles interrupted my thoughts. "Divers

can be out at 5 am tomorrow if weather permits, and they have three of the six available."

"That's great news," I replied with relief. "In the meantime, let's head down to the harbor and map out all the cameras within a 100-meter radius."

"I have a printout of all the known cameras on my desk," Henry offered as he grabbed them.

"Can you check with Li and see if she's free?" I asked Miles before making my way back to my desk.

About 30 minutes later, we were all ready to go. The air was thick with anticipation as we prepared for our mission. I paired Henry with Li, eager to check out all the cameras and possible dash cams in the underground car park. Meanwhile, Miles and I headed towards the harbor, the bustling sounds of a busy port filling our ears.

The dock was a maze of ships and shops, and we carefully navigated through it to see what cameras were listed on the printout and which were visible. We also wanted to scope out any cameras attached to nearby clubs or bars, hoping to find some not listed on the current form.

As we passed a newly opened club, Miles said, "That place would have a new camera installed."

"It's probably not open right now," I replied, reaching for my phone. "Let's see if we can get someone here to ask."

While Miles searched for a contact number, I couldn't shake off an overwhelming feeling of concern.

As I stared at my phone, I felt a pull to call Lily and ensure she was okay. Why did I feel so compelled to reach out to her? A sudden wave of fear washed over me, making my heart race.

I rubbed at my chest, where a strange sensation seemed to be pulsating. This feeling toward Lily wasn't something I was comfortable with. Before I could dwell on it further, Miles interrupted my thoughts.

"You okay?" he asked with raised eyebrows.

"I think so," I hesitated before confessing, "Just got a rush of fear and an urge to run to Lily."

Miles furrowed his brow in concern. "Rock, I don't think this is a good sign. She has to be your Mate...there's no other explanation for it."

"Fuck," I muttered as the tension in my body slowly subsided. "I'm not ready for a mate."

"I don't think we're meant to be," Miles shrugged. "I think we're just supposed to have it hit us one day, and then we'll have no choice but to embrace it."

"Well, that's just great," I sighed heavily. "We need to wrap this case up quickly. I can't afford to be distracted because of this. I'll have to keep my distance from her until it's over."

"Do you think distance is going to help?" Miles chuckled. "I've heard that the bonding begins once your body recognizes your mate. She'll start feeling your emotions, not hers, and the pull towards you will become irresistible."

His words struck a chord with me, causing another surge of unease throughout my body. "I know...which is why I'm worried right now. That fear I felt just now...it was intense."

"Is it gone now?" Miles asked, his voice filled with concern.

"Yes, I feel normal again; for all I know, a spider just jumped out at her and scared her. I can't just run off whenever I feel something strange; I have to wrap this up, then address it."

"Sounds like a plan," Miles states, ripping the paper sheet in his hand in half, "You take half, and I'll take half; let's mark them off and make sure they look like they are all working."

"Deal," I state, reaching out to grab my half.

As we make our way down the dock, I can't help but notice the multitude of cameras scattered around us. I quickly spot a few that aren't on our list and approach the storefront owners, requesting video footage from them. Unfortunately, only two shops have weekly recordings, while the rest only record daily and then overwrite the footage. These businesses have been on the docks for over a decade and likely didn't have the funds to update their security systems, especially after COVID-19.

So far, our search has yielded no useful information. We are left with more questions than answers.

Miles returned to me with even less progress than I had found. The cameras he had looked at from the side of the dock were spray-painted over and rendered useless. The new club only had downward-facing cameras above its doors, mainly monitoring patrons entering and exiting.

This investigation was like searching for a needle in a haystack. Each lead brought us closer to frustration rather than resolution.

12

After work, instead of heading home, I changed into some training gear, caught the light rail down to Haymarket, and walked a few blocks to John's gym. As I walked in, I looked around and was taken back to the first time I walked through these doors. I was a shadow of myself; every loud noise made me jump, and my anxiety was at an all-time high. But after months of training here, it completely changed my life; I still had a lot of work to do, and I wasn't completely ready, but I had learned enough to live life again and stop hiding in the shadows. This time, I was walking through these doors, finally ready to face my demons and put my past behind me once and for all.

"Lily," I heard John call my name and I turned towards him as he walked to me still standing at the front of the gym.

"Hi John," I said smiling as he wrapped his arms around me and pulled me into a hug. John was a very built man with shoulders for days, he reminded me of the Rock, all muscle with a bald head, and the kindest smile you have ever seen. When he smiled he smiled with his whole face and his brown eyes despite being as dark as night they were bright and kind. Do not get me wrong, if you pissed this guy off you definitely wouldn't want to come across him in a dark alley on your own, because I think he would end you in one punch. He was trained to kill, and I am sure he would if he had to but hey, I guess we all would if it came down to us or them.

"It's great to see you again kid," He whispered into my ear.

"You too John, You too," I stated relishing in the familiar embrace and comfort that I always got from John. John pulled away but kept his hands on my shoulders, "It's time," he stated his face all serious.

"It's time," I repeated his words nodding my head knowing it was the truth.

"Let's do this then," he replied squeezing my shoulder before letting go, turning and walking into the training room. I quickly followed behind him taking in the changes he had made in the time I had been gone.

As I walked into the training room I was greeted with 5 sets of eyes, all other women standing around in a half circle all here for the same self-defence classes I was here for.

"Ladies, This is Lily," John introduced me to the women as all their attention remained on me, "we will get to full introductions later" he added.

I waved at the women and they all waved back some smiling and others just turning back to John as he took his position in front of the room. I quickly walked towards the front of the room, put my stuff in the pigeon hole, kicked off my shoes, then moved to the mat and took my place.

"Today we are going to focus on getting past your fear," John announced to the class, looking along the line of women standing before him, "I am going to push your comfort zone and get you to really hone in your deepest darkest fears, so that if you are confronted with that fear, you don't freeze, you react because your fear no longer controls you," he said firmly, looking directly at me.

I gave a curt nod in understanding, and John continued the class.

"Let's get to work," John said, returning to the room as three other men entered. "This is Shane, Tom and Luke. They are going to help with today's class. They are well-trained, so don't be afraid to really give it your all with these exercises. We are going to split into pairs with one trainer to assist you, Lily and Jane. You two pair up with Luke," John directed as I turned to Jane to introduce myself.

"Hi, I'm Lily," I said, holding my hand to Jane.

"Nice to meet you, Lily. I'm Jane," she replied, shaking my hand softly. Jane looked to be in her 30s. She was petite, with strawberry-blonde hair and light blue eyes. Her nose and cheeks were covered in freckles, and she gave off a sweet and innocent vibe.

"Ladies," Luke said as he approached us, "I'm Luke, and I will be your trainer today. " He added, holding out his hand to Jane first. She quickly shook it, stating her name and released his hand just as quickly. Luke turned to me and held out his hand.

"Lily," I told him my name as I shook his hand and then pulled mine from his embrace.

"Nice to meet you both," Luke said, smiling. He was tall and well built—not as built as John, but he had wide shoulders, and you could see his biceps through his shirt, so he clearly worked out and did it regularly enough. He had sandy blonde hair, brown eyes and a charming edge. He was good-looking but nothing compared to Matt.

Shit, there I go again, referring and comparing every guy to Matt; I needed to get him out of my head.

"So today," Luke began, "I am literally going to come at you and keep coming at you. You are going to try and fend me off to your best ability. " He added, almost smirking, which actually really irritated me, but I pushed it aside.

"We need a safe word," Luke added, "just in case you reach your limit and need me to stop." This time, there was no smirk; he was serious and taking the safe word seriously. There was a stretch of silence, and I guessed he was waiting for our word.

"Red," I said almost in a whisper

"Great," Luke advised, "and you, Jane," he asked

"Umm, Purple, I guess," Jane said nervously as she rubbed her left arm with her right hand.

"Lily, would you like to go first," Luke asked me, gesturing towards the main training mat.

I looked towards Jane, and her eyes were almost pleading with me to say yes, so I did.

"Sure," I said, following Luke onto the mat. I took some deep breaths, trying to calm my nerves. "Just remember this isn't real. He won't hurt you," I told myself.

"You are going to close your eyes to the count of 10 and then open them, and it will begin," Luke advised on the instructions. Remember your safe word and use it if you need to," he added, looking me directly in the eyes so that I understood. I nodded.

"Ready?" Luke stated, and I closed my eyes and counted out loud to 10. I tried to hone in my senses like John had taught me previously; even counting, I could hear and sense Luke moving around me; as I got to 10 to open my eyes, I knew he was behind me. He was on me when I said ten and opened my eyes. I quickly stepped out of his way, ducking so that he couldn't grab at me; he flew past me, clearly putting a lot of power into that first move and not expecting me to be that fast. He quickly spun on his heels, charged at me faster than I expected, and grabbed me. I grabbed his arm, yanking it down towards the ground, and spun away from him again, moving out of his grasp.

"Not bad," Luke said as if taunting me as he quickly recovered, spinning around to face me. We went around like this for a few more minutes, him lunging and trying to grab me and me using all the skills I had learned to get out of his grasp. Still, Luke seemed to be getting smarter and was learning my moves; on my next attempt to elbow him in the ribs as he came up behind me, he quickly moved to the side, and I missed him, giving him the perfect timing to grab my lowered arm and spin it up behind my back pinning it there. Then he quickly kicked the back of my knees with his foot, and I fell to the ground as Luke still held my arm behind me; as I hit the ground fully, he straddled my back and pushed me onto the mat. I tried my hardest to get out of his hold, but panic was kicking in. My heart was beating fast as a flashback reminded me of the time I was in a similar position only I didn't have a safe word to get me out. My attacker had me pinned and was trying to cut off my air supply, and there was nothing I could do about it.

"Safeword!" I heard someone say as I snapped back to reality and realized I was in panic mode. My breath was fast and shallow, and my eyes were filled with tears at the memory I had just had.

"Red," I called out. Luke immediately let me go and moved off me, and I quickly sat up, trying to catch my breath.

"Deep breaths," John said, coming to sit next to me as I took his instruction and tried to take a deep breath while wiping away the tears that had rolled down my cheeks.

"You're okay," John said, taking my hands that I hadn't even realised were shaking into his to comfort me. It did. I began to take full, deep breaths, and my heart rate slowly calmed.

"Whatever happened in that moment, that's the fear you need to control; that's the fear you need to break," John said, looking into my eyes as if he were looking into my soul.

"He almost killed me," I stated out of nowhere, shocking myself a little, but clearly, it needed to come out; another single tear rolled down my cheek, but I quickly wiped it away.

"But he didn't," John stated very matter-of-factly, and he was right; my attacker hadn't killed me; I was still here on this earth, and I needed to stop letting this fear control me.

13

After a few hours of combing the docks, I returned to the office and knocked on Sam's door. "Rock, what can I do for you?" Sam asked as I entered.

"I need to have a quick chat," I told him.

"Is this about the girl?" Sam frowned at me.

"Yes," I replied, "I believe she is my mate, but I don't want to be taken off the case. I'll have Miles take over with her while I maintain some distance until things are sorted out."

"You know it would be best if we just took you off the case completely," Sam sighed. "Why do you think she is your mate anyway? What made you realize this?" he asked.

"Well, today I had this overwhelming fear and a strong urge to shift and run to Lily," I admitted.

Sam smirked and said, "Yep, that would do it. Congratulations on finding your mate, Rock." He beamed at me.

"I'm not sure I'm ready for congratulations just yet," I grumbled. "I wasn't ready for a mate, and I wasn't even looking."

"You're not going to reject your mate, are you?" Sam looked at me with disgust.

"No way!" I exclaimed. "She's mine, and there's no question about it. I want to wrap up this case before taking time off to sort things out."

"You do realize that staying away from her won't solve anything?" Sam responded with a hint of disapproval.

I sighed hesitantly and responded, "I know, but I'm hoping it will provide some temporary relief while we finish." My words are met with a chuckle from Sam.

"The pull might become too strong, and the next time she gets startled by a spider, it could trigger the change no matter where you are," he laughs. "One time, Jane was watering the garden at home. As she watered one of the Magnolia bushes, a tiny Garden snake slithered out and scared her half to death. I was on a ladder at the time, taking down Christmas lights. The change came over me instantly, and I fell off the ladder on my hind legs. Luckily, no one saw it happen, but Jane never let me live it down." A hint of sadness crosses Sam's face as he remembers his late mate.

She had passed away two years ago in a tragic car accident caused by a drunk driver. She died instantly, her wolf healing and strength not standing a chance against the impact to be able to help her. The driver was sent to jail and has since turned sober. Sam took it upon himself to become his sponsor and ensure that he stayed sober for the rest of his life.

I can't help but wonder how Sam could forgive the man when I would have wanted nothing more than revenge. But Sam believes that this is what Jane would have wanted him to do - to look after the man and help him get his life back together.

"So what do you think we should do, Alpha?" I ask, still unsure of the best course of action.

"Maybe it's time we give Miles the lead role, and you take a step back," Sam suggests calmly. "You'll still be a part of the team, but let Miles run things for now."

The suggestion hung in the air, a lifeline for me to still fulfill my duties and sort out my personal life. I couldn't help but smile at the thought.

"Sounds like a plan," I reply, trying to hide my relief.

"We'll limit your contact with Ms James while on the job. If you pursue her outside of work, it's none of my concern," Sam says firmly.

"Understood," I nod.

"Someone will have to inform her office about her colleague and also contact Lily to let her know that she was acquainted with the victim," I suggest, sinking back into the chair across from Sam's desk.

"Good idea. Get Li on it," Sam agrees. "And stay away from her until she knows."

"Got it," I say as I rise from my seat.

"Is that all for today?" Sam asks.

Just as I stand, a bolt of fear shoots through my chest, causing me to double over and clutch my stomach as if I'm about to be sick. The change is coming, marked by the tingling in my feet.

"Stop!" Sam's alpha voice cuts through me, halting my shift.

"She's scared!" I blurt out, frantically trying to rush out the door.

"Stop!" Sam's alpha command echoes again, forcing my feet to stop their panicked movements.

"What are you feeling?" Sam growls at me.

"Fear. Bone-crushing fear, gripping onto my soul," I answer without hesitation. If Lily is experiencing this same type of fear, something is very wrong.

"Is it still present now?" He asks me

"Yes, but not as bad as it first was. It's getting less and less." I answer while rubbing my sternum.

"Can you sense her location?"

"Yes, she feels like she is that way, I state, pointing to the left of me, towards Chinatown."

"Is the fear still gripping you?" Sam asked.

"No, it's barely there now," I say back.

"Good, hopefully, it was just a spider," Sam said. Stood walked to his door and opened it. Leaning out, he yelled, "Miles, get in here," and walked back to his seat.

"Rock sit down," He asked.

Sitting back down, I rubbed my sternum; that fear that ran through me was all-consuming. What the hell was going on with Lily? What was scaring her so much?

"Alpha?" Miles states as he walks in the door and closes it behind him.

"Sit, Miles," Sam points to the chair beside mine.

Taking a seat next to me Miles notes me rubbing my chest.

"Again," he asks.

"Yes, but worse this time."

"Miles, you're taking the lead on this case," Sam explains. "Rock is going to have a more mentoring role, than a role at all. Lily is his mate; we can't have him wolfing out on us every 2 seconds."

"Yes Alpha," Miles answers back.

"Organise for Li to go to Ms James' workplace tomorrow

to inform them about the co-worker's death. I also want you to find Ms James today and inform her personally about the co-worker and find out where she has been today," Sam asked Miles.

"Yes, Alpha," he replied.

"We need to get to the bottom of this now. The whole Mate issue will be a bigger mess than planned," Sam points at me.

"You need to go home, go for a run, and work off some of this steam. Miles will call you once he has located and informed Ms James. Hopefully, she will tell him where she has been so we can get a handle on this fear issue."

"Yes, Alpha," I reply.

I needed to get on top of this. There would have been too many questions if I had shifted here in the office and run out with my fluffy tail. I needed to find out what was going on with Lily, but I also needed to follow orders from my alpha.

All my wolf kept saying to me was MINE!

14

This afternoon was tough, but it was something that I needed to do, and I was ready to embrace whatever feelings the sessions were going to rehash. After today's session, John reassured me that I was strong enough to face whatever was thrown at me. He was right. I had grown so much in the last twelve months and started to take back ownership of my life, so now was the perfect time to face my past and fears and wholeheartedly take control of my future.

I saw a guy leaning against the wall as I approached my front gate. He wore trousers, a work shirt and a tie, and his face looked familiar. I couldn't pick where I knew him from. I had a feeling that whoever he was waiting for was me. As I got closer, he spotted me and smiled, which made me relax a little, but not 100%.

"Ms James," he addressed me. He had a nice smile and some seriously white and straight teeth. His eyes were hazel, his hair was blonde, and his whole demeanor was relaxed, like he knew who I was and felt comfortable with me.

"Hi," I said hesitantly raising a brow as I still tried to work out how I knew this guy.

"Detective Miles," he said, introducing himself and clueing me into where I had seen him before. He worked with Matt and was one of the detectives from the day that I found the body floating in the harbor.

"How can I help you, detective?" I asked as I reached into my bag and pulled out my keys, not taking my eyes off him.

"I was hoping that we would be able to speak; I have an update on the case," Detective Miles informed me.

"Oh," I said, not expecting that. But what did I expect a detective to advise me? I guess I was just surprised that Matt wasn't here himself.

"Sorry, I thought Detective Rocklan was in charge of the case," I added, trying to cover up my disappointment that Matt wasn't here.

"Rock's still helping out with the case; I am just taking the lead on this one," Detective Miles advised me with a sly little smirk as if he saw my disappointment that he was here and not Matt.

"Right, ok, well, did you want me to come to the station," I asked.

"You could, or if there is somewhere we could talk in private where you would be more comfortable," Detective Miles informed me.

"Sure, we could go up to my apartment?" I suggested moving to unlock the gate.

"That would be great," Miles advised.

We both made our way to my apartment pretty much in silence, apart from me meeting my neighbor as we passed in the hall. When we got inside, I felt a little uneasy, as no man had ever been in there before, and the one man I would want was not here.

"Would you like a drink or anything?" I asked nervously as I sat my stuff down on the chair at the dining table.

"No, I am fine, thank you though," Detective Miles stated smiling, "Would you like to take a seat," he added gesturing towards the nearest dining seat to me.

"Yes, of course," I said, moving the seat out. "Please sit if you would like," I added to Detective Miles as I sat. He followed suit, taking a seat on the opposite side of me but keeping his chair at an angle so that he could keep one leg on the other side of the table.

I sighed deeply before asking, "So, what is that update?" I started looking Detective Miles in the eye.

"We have identified the man you found floating in the harbor, and I am sorry to advise that it is your co-worker, Ryan Smalls," Detective Miles informed me.

With those words, the room blurred, my mind went blank and ringing in my ears started as the panic began to set in.

My chest began to tighten, and I could feel my breath quicken. No matter how hard I tried to breathe, I could not catch my breath. Detective Miles was at my side within a split second, anticipating my reaction.

"It's okay, Ms. James. Just breathe," he kept repeating, but it wasn't helping.

Ryan was dead, my co-worker was dead, and I had found him; my mind was racing, and flashbacks of my past were running through my mind; it was happening again.

"Lily, look at me," Detective Miles yelled at me, bringing my attention back to him as I looked him directly in the eyes. Breath," he said, "Just like what I am doing, in slowly through your nose, out through your mouth," he stated as I watched him and followed his direction.

"Again," he said, and again, I followed his directions, in slowly through my nose and out slowly through my mouth. I kept doing this until I could feel the panic fade away, and everything came back into focus.

"Are you OK?" Detective Miles asked, not taking his eyes off me. His look of concern was heartwarming; I could see that he was honestly concerned about my welfare.

"Yes, Thank you," I confirmed, nodding slightly to reassure him with more than words. As I looked down, I noticed that at some point, he must have moved my chair to turn me around to face him, and he was kneeling in front of me but not touching me.

He began to stand up and put some space between us as he spoke, "Ok, good. I think Rock would kill me if anything happened to you," Detective Miles stated, his eyes going wide as if noting he had said it out loud before he added, "You know, because Rock takes everyone's safety very seriously."

I looked at Detective Miles for a moment, trying to figure out if what he had said was because Matt had spoken about me and felt this weird pull to me like I had to him.

"Did you know Mr Smalls very well?" Detective Miles asked me, bringing my thoughts back to the present and reminding me that the body I had found in the harbor was Ryan.

"Not really," I answered, "We were co-workers, and we had hung out in a group before after work a few times," I added, wringing my hands.

"Was there any sort of romantic interest between you?" he asked me

"Umm, well, not on my end. Ryan had asked me out a couple of times, but I just wasn't interested in him like that," I answered.

"Hmm," Detective Miles murmured.

"But he was fine with it," I added quickly, not wanting it to sound like there was a grudge between us. "There were never any issues between us,"

"Any other person in your life that would be unhappy with Ryan asking you out?" He asked next

"As in a boyfriend? No, no one," I answered, but something in Detective Miles' expression made me think he didn't believe me. I didn't say anything to defend myself. Then it hit me.

"Wait, you think someone killed Ryan? It wasn't just a horrible accident; you think someone hated him enough that they killed him!" I started, shocked and confused, "Why would anyone want to hurt Ryan? He was a nice enough guy; he didn't seem like the type of guy that would have any enemies."

"It does look like foul play in the case of Mr Ryan," Detective Miles answered, seeming sympathetic to my reaction.

"I just cannot believe anyone would want to hurt Ryan," I said, still in complete shock. Thoughts began to run through my head. Did this have something to do with me? Was it set up so that I was the one to find him, or was that just a coincidence? Matt had said that the woman who was killed had a resemblance to me, Were the 2 cases linked?

"Penny for your thoughts," Detective Miles asked.

"My mind is racing; none of this seems real," I advised him, shaking my head and looking down at my hands.

"It's a lot to take in, I know," Detective Miles said, "but

know that we are doing everything we can to get to the bottom of what happened to Mr Smalls."

"I don't know what to say in this situation; thank you, I guess, is about all I can come up with," I said, trying to smile at him, but I was just unable to accomplish it.

Detective Miles smiled at me, "Well, I'd better be going, but if you remember anything else or if you need anything, please feel free to call me at any time." He added, reaching into his pocket, pulling out a card and handing it to me.

"I will thank you," I said, taking the card and standing up to let him out of my apartment.

After he had left, I closed the door and leaned against it, sinking to the ground and hugging my legs.

"Please, God, don't let Ryan's death be because of me," I said almost in a whisper as I closed my eyes and prayed.

15

DETECTIVE MATTHEW ROCKLAN

Sitting on the worn leather couch in my cramped apartment, I slurped up a spoonful of steaming ramen noodles. Suddenly, a sharp tingle shot through my toes, and my canines began to ache. I clenched my fists and focused on slow, deep breaths, trying to suppress my transformation.

My phone pinged earlier with a text from Miles, letting me know he was at her apartment. I felt a wave of relief wash over me, knowing that she was not in any immediate danger. But the sense of panic still lingered, fuelled by the shock and grief of her co-worker's unexpected passing. It was not the typical reaction one would expect from someone who had just lost a colleague; this was a deep-seated fear bubbling back up to the surface. The kind that leaves your heart racing and your palms sweaty, unable to shake off the feeling of impending doom.

Lily seemed to hold secrets close to her chest, like a treasure she was unwilling to share. I knew I needed to uncover them. Miles had promised to text me after he left her apartment and urged me to talk to her afterward. At the time, I hesitated - unsure if it was wise. But now, an unshakeable feeling tugged at my gut, compelling me to go. My wolf was on edge now, and I could feel the lingering sensation of fear still pumping through my veins from Lily.

Placing my unfinished ramen noodles in the fridge to eat later, I quickly jump into the shower. Miles will be texting me soon, and I wanted to head out the second he did.

My muscles twitched as I stepped into the shower, my mind racing with the urge to shift. I felt the warm water flow over my body as I stepped under it. I was trying to get my mind to calm down. Grabbing my body wash I went to work cleaning away the dirt from the day.

When I was done, I stepped out of the warm shower, quickly grabbing my towel to wipe away the moisture from my skin. As I walked towards the mirror, drops of water trailed down my body and pooled on the bathroom floor. My gaze fell upon my reflection, and I couldn't help but notice the intricate web of scars that adorned my torso. They were souvenirs from work. But even with our advanced healing abilities, scars remained. Four stood out prominently - three bullet wound scars scattered across my upper torso and a long, jagged scar running down my back from a deep stab wound. I had always hoped that women found scars attractive, as these marks were impossible to hide when I was shirtless.

I hastily slip on clothes and grab my phone off the table. My heart quickened at the sight of a missed call from Miles, and I eagerly pressed the green button below his name to return his call.

"Rock," Miles said. "I thought you'd surely be glued to your phone like usual."

"Haha, very funny," I reply sarcastically. "I was taking a shower."

"Good, I suggest you head over to her place; she is gonna need someone," He says with a sad tone.

"She didn't take it well, which I'm sure you felt, but I heard her whisper, 'Please God, don't let Ryan's death be because of me.' as I was walking away, there was something important she wasn't telling us," he states.

With a heavy sigh, I reluctantly admit, "I know, I feel the same way." Without exchanging any further pleasantries, I abruptly hang up the phone and quickly gather my belongings - keys, wallet - from the bench as I make my way out the door.

As I head down to my car, I can already feel the tension building in my shoulders. Lily's apartment was only a 15-minute drive from mine, but it could easily turn into a 30-minute ordeal during rush hour traffic. Sitting in bumper-to-bumper cars for that long makes me want to scream.

I finally reach my beat-up Honda and journey towards Lily's place. As expected, the roads are congested with cars and impatient drivers. Despite my best efforts to navigate the sea of vehicles, it took me 40 minutes to reach her apartment today. A major accident on the road forced everything to condense into one lane. When were dickheads going to learn to drive?

My wolf had been restless and on edge for hours, his presence a constant hum in the back of my mind. The gear shift at the office was one thing, but this afternoon brought a heightened need to lay eyes on my mate. Every nerve in my body was buzzing with anticipation, my skin prickling with excitement. I couldn't wait to lay eyes on her again.

Thankfully, there was a park on the road just three doors up from Lily's apartment complex. Parking my car, I jumped out and walked up to the gate surrounding the building.

With a button press, I heard Lily's voice flow through the speakers, soft and melodic. It caressed my ears like a gentle breeze on a warm summer day. "Hello," she says. I held down the intercom button and responded, "Lily, it's Matt." Her name rolls off my tongue like a familiar song. "Detective Rocklan?" She clarifies, her voice tinged with surprise. I nod instinctively before realizing she can't see me. I turn my face towards the camera pointed down at me so she can see my features on the intercom screen, hoping to ease her doubts or fears.

"What can I do for you, Matt?" She asks, her voice soft and melodic.

Heart racing, I reply, "Can I come up?" There is a moment of tense silence before she responds.

I second-guessed my question, feeling the panic rise in my chest. But just as I was about to retract it, the gate buzzed, granting me entry. With haste, I pushed open the gate and made my way to her unit. Making sure to close the gate properly behind me, I took deep breaths to calm my nerves.

After a short walk, I finally reached her door and knocked eagerly. It only took 30 seconds for her to answer, but it felt like an eternity. She opened the door, dressed in black lounge pants and an oversized soft blue top that hung off one shoulder. Her beautiful brown hair was pulled up in a messy bun on top of her head, and she wore the ugliest fluffy socks I have ever seen. Despite this, she still managed to look effortlessly stunning.

I speak up, breaking the tense silence between us. "Hello," I say, my voice echoing off the walls of her small apartment.

Her expression softened as she met my gaze. "Can I come in?" I raised my eyebrows at her, silently pleading for entrance.

She stood there, speechless for a moment before finally

responding. "Um, shit, yes." She moved aside to hold the door open wider, allowing me to slip past her and into the dimly lit living room.

"What can I do for you, Matt?" she asked, closing the door softly behind us. Her eyes are hesitant and guarded.

"Detective Miles was here an hour ago," she adds.

"Yes, I know, he rang me after he left," I admit.

I felt a little sick with nerves, wondering how I was going to tell her she was my mate. Should I have not told her and just let it progress naturally?

Sam had warned me that keeping this information from her could lead to even more trouble if she found out alone. I debated whether to reveal it or let things progress naturally between us.

"Ok, what did you need to talk to me about then?" She asked, her eyebrows furrowed in concern.

"It's more than just talking; I need to tell you something," I admitted, my heart racing with anticipation.

"I know about Ryan if that's what you're here for," she said softly, her tone understanding.

I gesture to myself and then to her, the words tumbling out of my mouth quickly. "No, I'm here to tell you about us."

She looked at me with curiosity and confusion. "Um, okay," she said uncertainly.

"Did you wanna sit down?" Her hand gestured towards a plush, white couch in the corner of the room.

"Yes, that might be a good idea," I replied, feeling my body tense as I sank into the soft cushions.

"I need to explain something to you," I begin, choosing my words carefully. "You are my Mate."

16

LILY JAMES

"You are my Mate," The words rang in my ears, did I just hear him correctly, did Matt just say he was my mate, mate like some fantasy novel of what, shifters and paranormal activity or something? Was he being serious or was this just some sort of joke? I looked at him still trying to get a read on the situation as I took a seat down next to him.

"Is this some sort of joke?" I asked staring at him in disbelief but I still sat there not wanting to move away from him and feeling the connection to him that I had from the moment I saw him.

"It's not a joke at all," Matt said his face serious with a hint of what looked to be sadness.

"Think about it," he went on to say, "You feel a pull to me and you have no idea why, we don't know each other but I am always on your mind and the few interactions we have had, there has been this attraction between us that is so strong it's hard to walk away or forget about it afterwards."

I sat there staring at Matt for a while, he wasn't wrong all those things were true, I mean even now when logically in my mind after what he said I should be laughing in his face and telling him to get out but here I was sitting, not running for the hills. But surely what we were feeling towards each other was just sexual chemistry and attraction, not some supernatural power or whatever he was referring to. Mates were the things I read about in fantasy novels, like Destiny and Werewolves and Twilight crap and this was real life, not some fantasy or a movie.

"You're feeling overwhelmed," Matt stated his head tilting slightly to the side as he watched me with pleading eyes. I wanted to believe what he was saying I did, but it just didn't make any sense.

"I know this is a lot, and I need you to know, I feel all those things too." Matt looks at me with pleading eyes.

"You are always on my mind, and I feel this need to protect you," Matt stated reaching out to rest his hand on mine and I let him, needing him to reassure me, needing to feel his touch. I looked down at our hands and then back up to look into his eyes.

"Matt I…" I started to say but he cut me off.

"You don't need to say anything right now," Matt said standing up and pulling me up with him so we were standing in front of each other still holding hands.

I looked up into his eyes and he looked into mine. We stood there staring at each other and a warmth spread through my body making me feel safe and protected, something I had not felt in a long time, deep down I knew it was Matt who was giving that to me. My heart wanted to tell him everything and run off into the sunset but my head was screaming at me to protect myself, to wake up and smell the roses and stop dreaming.

"I can't do this," I said pulling away from Matt and walking towards my door, halfway there I spun around and Matt was right behind me.

"Do you know how crazy this sounds," I said waving my hands around at him as I stepped back putting some space between us again, "you want me to believe that we're mates, like some supernatural, destiny of what, the moon gods or something? That shit is make-believe and makes a great read but it's not reality! I mean do you expect me to believe that you also shift into a wolf, a bear, a jaguar I mean come on Matt, You're a detective in the Australian Police Force!" I said "Are you not meant to be mentally stable to get that position," I ranted at him as my mind ran a thousand miles an hour.

Matt raised his eyebrows and a chuckle escaped his mouth "This isn't funny Matt," I said folding my arms over my chest and stomping my foot in frustration.

"I know this isn't funny," Matt replied taking a step closer to me, "and the fact that you haven't started running for the hills means that you feel this thing between us as much as I do, and for the record, I'm a shifter, wolf to be exact," he added taking another step forward and closing the gap between us.

"It's just not possible," I stated looking up at him referring to the fact that he was claiming to be a shifter and not the part about me feeling the attraction and pull between us.

"What if it is just our destiny," Matt stated so matter of fact as he looked at me lovingly.

Matt's words immediately took me back to one of the scariest nights of my life, a night that changed my life forever.

It was dark and raining and I was the only one home when I heard a noise. When I looked out the window I saw him standing there in the rain just staring at the house and the hairs stood up on alert all over my body as a chill ran over me. It was dark both inside the house and outside but I knew he could see me as much as I could see him. I went to reach for my phone when it began to ring and without thinking I picked it up. I was met with heavy breathing and the sound of rain and knew it was him. "You will be mine, No one can keep us apart, you belong to me, I am your destiny."

"Lily," Matt's voice cut through my flashback bringing me back to the present. He was caressing my cheek and when I looked up into his eyes there was so much concern there it almost broke my heart as I knew what I had to do.

"Get out," I yelled pushing him away and he stumbled back clearly not expecting my actions or my strength.

"Lily what's wrong," Matt asked going to move towards me.

"Stop," I yelled stopping him in his tracks, "I am not anyone's destiny, I don't belong to anyone," I stated a single tear rolling down my cheek and I quickly wiped it away.

"Lily, it's ok," Matt said with his hands raised in the air as if surrendering

"Please leave," I said sternly as he looked at me with sad eyes

"Ok," Matt said lowering his hands and standing up straight, "I will leave, but know that I am here for you, always," he stated his lips almost quivering as he turned and walked towards the door. He opened it and stepped out but turned around to face me again.

"I am not giving up on us Lily James," he stated with a smile and then turned and left.

17

DETECTIVE MATTHEW ROCKLAN

The door slammed with a force that reverberated through my bones, leaving me standing in the dimly lit hallway of Lily's apartment building, reeling from what had just transpired. I could still feel the sting in my chest as her piercing green eyes bore into mine, the anger and confusion swirling within them. The echo of her voice rang in my ears, harsh and biting, "Please leave!"

I leaned against the wall, trying to make sense of it all. Was it the fact that I'd admitted we were mates? The mere mention of the word seemed to send her into a frenzy. Or was it because she realised I was serious, and there was no denying that I was a shifter? There was a palpable tension between us, an invisible thread that connected our hearts – one that I knew she felt too, whether she admitted it or not.

Or maybe it was me saying we were destined to be together. It sounded so sure, so final, and maybe that scared her. As much as I wanted to protect her from the dangers that lurked in the shadows, I couldn't help but wonder if I was bringing them closer instead.

My fingers traced the outline of the door, feeling the coarse wood beneath my fingertips. I was tempted to knock, to try and explain myself once more, but I knew that for now, it was best to let her have her space. She needed time to process everything.

With a heavy sigh, I pushed myself away from the wall and made my way towards the exit. My steps echoed in the empty hallway, each thud a reminder of the distance growing between us. As I reached for the handle, I paused, glancing back at Lily's door one last time.

As I stepped out into the night, the cool breeze brushed against my skin, sending a shiver down my spine. The city's cacophony of sounds enveloped me – the distant laughter of people enjoying their night out, the hum of traffic on the street below, the occasional honk of a car horn.

But all of it seemed insignificant, drowned out by the thoughts that consumed me. What had set her off? What would it take to bridge the gap between us and mend the rift that threatened to tear us apart?

I knew one thing for certain – giving up was not an option. I would fight for Lily, for us, until my last breath left my body. Because when you find your mate, your other half, nothing else matters more than holding onto them and never letting go.

The streetlights cast a harsh yellow glow on the wet pavement, reflecting distorted images that seemed to echo my fractured thoughts. My heart felt heavy in my chest, but I didn't have time to dwell on it now. I had to find a way to get her to open up to me, even if she wanted nothing to do with me.

I pulled out my phone and sent her a text message before starting the engine. "No matter what, call me any day or time. I'll always be here for you." I hesitated for a moment, my finger hovering above the 'send' button, before finally pressing it. It was all I could do for now.

"Damn it, Lily," I muttered under my breath as I eased the car into traffic and headed home. "Can't you feel this pull like I can?"

My apartment building loomed ahead, it's brick facade somehow both comforting and imposing all at once. As I parked out front, the weight of the night's events pressed down on me like a physical force. I couldn't shake the feeling that something terrible was about to happen, and I needed to be ready.

Just as I stepped out of my car, my phone buzzed in my pocket. I pulled it out to see Sam, calling me. A sense of dread washed over me; it was never good news when Sam called this late.

"Rock," he said without preamble, his voice tense and low. "We've got another body. Same MO – female, looks just like Lily."

My blood ran cold and my fists clenched involuntarily. Another one? How many more would there be until the killer was satisfied? How long until it was Lily lying there lifeless?

"Where?" I asked, my voice barely above a growl.

"Down by the harbour. I've got the team headed there now." Sam paused for a moment, and I could almost see him weighing his words carefully. "I know you're struggling with the whole mate issue, Rock, but you need to keep your head on straight. We'll get this bastard."

"Thanks, Alpha," I muttered, trying to keep the anger out of my voice. But it was useless; the rage and frustration bubbled up inside me like molten lava, threatening to spill over and scorch everything in its path.

"Rock, do I need to completely pull you off this case?" Sam said.

"No," I growled, "I need to see it through now."

"Ok, we'll get down to the harbour, Miles is waiting to boss you around," he said and hung up.

My thoughts raced with questions and fears, but one thing remained clear – I had to protect Lily at all costs even if it meant defying my alpha if it came down to it.

As I headed down to the harbor, the salty breeze whipped at my face, reminding me that I was no longer in control. The moon was high in the sky, glowing the water. It would be strange taking orders from Miles, instead of calling the shots like I used to.

"Rock," a familiar voice called out. It was Henry, who had his sandy blonde hair styled.

"Hey, Henry," I raised my brows at his hair and pointed at it, trying to sound casual. "Nice hair...What's the situation?"

Henry smiled "I was on a date, but duty calls and all, but It's not good, Rock. Miles will fill you in."

I approached Miles, who stood solemnly by a bench over-looking the water. The rest of the team was scattered about, collecting evidence and talking in hushed tones. The air was thick with tension, and I could feel the weight of their collective anxiety pressing down on me.

"Rock," Miles greeted me with a nod.

My voice was tight "What've we got?"

Miles hesitated for a moment before gesturing to the bench. There, propped up as if she were enjoying the view, was a dead girl who looked just like Lily. My heart clenched in my chest, and I tried not to think about the last time I'd seen her.

"Strangled," Miles said quietly. "And there's... this." He handed me a note, scrawled in a twisted, menacing hand. It read: She is mine, not yours, Detective Rocklan.

"Son of a bitch," I muttered under my breath. Rage bubbled up inside me, threatening to spill over, but I forced it down.

"Who discovered her?" I inquired, my voice straining to remain steady.

"A man and his dog," Miles responded in a weary tone.

Why does it always have to be a man and his loyal canine companion? "Did they find anything?" I asked, struggling to control the primal instincts of my wolf who was determined to protect his mate- whether she wanted me or not.

Inhaling deeply, I forced myself to focus on the present situation at hand.

"Alright," I said firmly, pushing my personal feelings aside for the moment. "Let's get to work."

18

LILY JAMES

I tried to sleep but I just couldn't, everything that Matt had told me just kept rolling through my head. My overreaction to what he had said kept replaying in my mind and the look on his face when I asked him to leave was haunting me. I had hurt him and his pain made me feel a deep, sharp pain in my chest and every time I saw the pained look in his eyes the pain would return.

It was after midnight and I knew I was never going to get to sleep with all this running through my mind and the one thing that I knew always cleared it was a run. I got up and got changed into my running gear, I put my hair up into a messy bun, grabbed my headphones and phone next to my bed and set up my running music. Then I went out into the living area and grabbed my keys and off I went.

The streets were quiet at this time, there were a few people out walking around, but mostly the streets were empty. I loved to run at this time, with no one getting in my way it's just you, the pavement and the music in your ears helping to set the pace. I set my watch and then I was off, setting a nice pace as I tried not to think about everything that had happened over the last few days. Honestly, it felt like months had passed and I was so drained by it all, drained and scared to death that my past was coming back to haunt me.

I was about 30 minutes into my run and was getting close to the harbour when the hairs on the back of my neck stood to attention, a cold shiver ran down my spine, I knew someone was watching me and that feeling stopped me in my tracks. I ripped the headphones still playing my music, off my head and began to take in my surroundings as I looked around to see if I could see anyone.

Some of the office buildings were still well-lit but some were in complete darkness, the wind had picked up from when I started my run and the trees were rustling in the wind and I could hear an alarm going off in the distance. I spun on the spot checking in all directions to make sure that no one was going to sneak up on me. A loud bang sounded behind me, I jumped and screamed as I turned quickly in its direction but it was just a roadwork sign that had fallen over with the wind. I was starting to allow the panic to creep up.

No, you are not letting the fear take over I told myself as I started to take some calming deep breaths, I was not going to allow myself to be consumed by this, I had had enough. I looked around and saw police lights flashing down near the harbour, and something told me that my safety was in that direction, so without even second guessing it, I took off running towards the police lights. I knew whoever had been watching me was following me, I sensed their presence in every fibre of my being but I just kept running.

Just get to safety, I kept telling myself as I ran faster and faster, the adrenaline kicking in and pushing my body to a whole other level, it was fight or flight mode and this was me fighting for my life and I knew deep down inside that it was exactly that.

I was so close, I could hear people talking and the lights were flashing so bright and that's when I saw him, Matt and like a moth to a flame I ran straight for him, I ran straight to my safety.

He saw me before I reached him as if sensing me and something I could not read washed over his face. He was already running towards me with Miles and Henry right behind him. I didn't even see them when I spotted Matt, but there they were as if they had appeared out of thin air. Matt reached me first and I pretty much smashed into him as I was not able to stop in time but he didn't even flinch.

"Lily, you ok?" Matt asked as he wrapped his arms around me just as Miles and Henry took off straight past us.

I was breathing heavily and trying to suck in as much air as I could with Matt wrapped around me, but I didn't want to push him away, he was my safety and him being here tonight had saved my life and whatever the connection we had to each other it drew me to him, even before I realised I was in danger. I had never run that route before, I usually go in the completely other direction, but something drew me in this direction and now I knew that something was Matt.

"I could feel your panic," Matt whispered in my ear, "I was coming to find you but you found me," Matt stated pulling away and cupping my face.

"Someone was following me," I managed to get out in between breaths.

"I know," Matt stated, "Lily he was right behind you, Henry and Miles took off after him,"

"What?" I stated in complete shock my legs giving out a little but Matt steadied me. "He.. He was right behind me?" he had almost caught me, if Matt, Henry and Miles hadn't seen him and chased after him, maybe he would have caught me.

"You're safe now Lily," Matt assured me pulling me back into his embrace, "I will never let anyone hurt you," he whispered in my ear holding me a little closer. I believed him but he didn't know what he was up against, I knew I couldn't hide my past any longer, He was back whether I was ready for it or not he had somehow found me.

19

The fear etched into Lily's face as she sprinted towards me sent a jolt of terror through my veins. My heart thundered in my chest, and I could feel the urgent pounding of adrenaline coursing through me. Who, or what, was chasing her? With our shifter eyesight, we could all see the dark figure relentlessly pursuing Lily as she raced towards us on the dock.

The fear that had been simmering inside her just moments ago was what alerted me to something being terribly wrong in the first place. That's why Miles, Henry, and I were charging towards her when she finally spotted us.

I pushed myself harder to close the distance between us. My muscles burned with the push.

"Lily, you ok?" I started as I wrapped my arms around her just as Miles and Henry took off straight past us.

My arms were tightly wrapped around Lily, her heart pounding wildly against my chest. I tried to calm the storm of emotions swirling within me – her fear, my own protective instincts – hoping that my presence would help soothe her as well. Her breath hitched, and she clung to me like a lifeline.

"I could feel your panic," I murmured into her hair, breathing in the sweet scent of her shampoo. "I was coming to find you but you found me."

"Someone was following me," she whispered, voice cracking.

"I know" I stated, "Lily he was right behind you, Henry and Miles took off after him."

As we stood there, I couldn't help but keep an eye on the darkness where Miles and Henry had disappeared. Despite their strength and confidence, I worried for their safety. Shadows seemed to shift and dance, taunting me with the unknown dangers they could conceal. My ears strained for any sign of struggle or alarm that might signal trouble.

"What?" she stated in complete shock her legs giving out a little but I managed to steady her. "He.. He was right behind me?" she stammered out

"You're safe now Lily," I assured her pulling her back into my embrace, "I will never let anyone hurt you," I whispered in her ear.

"Are they going to be alright?" Lily asked, following my gaze into the darkness.

"Of course," I reassured her, though I couldn't shake the uneasiness gnawing at me. "Miles and Henry are strong. They can handle themselves."

A powerful, familiar presence washed over me, and I instantly knew who it was – Sam. He appeared at my side like a silent guardian, his strong stance grounding me in the chaos of the night. I felt reassured by his presence, though I couldn't help but feel a pang of guilt for not having been more vigilant.

"Are you ok?" Sam's deep voice carried an undercurrent of

concern as he addressed Lily, his gaze never leaving the darkness where Miles and Henry had disappeared.

"Y-yes," Lily stammered, still clinging to me for support. "Thank you."

Sam then turned to me, his piercing eyes searching for answers. "Rock, did you see who was chasing her?"

I shook my head, frustration gnawing at me. "No, I only saw the figure, he was too far away to catch a proper sight of. I'm hoping Miles or Henry saw something."

"Let's hope so," Sam muttered, his jaw clenched with worry. If he already knew this much, it meant that one of the boys must have shifted during the chase and communicated with him.

"Welcome to the pack, Lily," Sam said, suddenly extending a hand towards her. His voice softened, betraying the gentle soul beneath his imposing exterior. "I'm the Alpha. I know you're probably very confused right now, but Rock here will explain everything to you - the whole pack laws and everything you need to know."

Lily hesitated for a moment before cautiously placing her shaking hand in his. As she did so, I could sense the warmth radiating from both of them, their connection forming the first threads of a bond that would only grow stronger over time.

"Thank you," she whispered, her voice barely audible above the sound of waves crashing against the shore. It was clear that she was still shaken and afraid.

"Alright," Sam said, releasing Lily's hand and casting one last glance into the darkness. "We'll wait for Miles and Henry to return. Rock, stay with Lily"

"Of course," I agreed, tightening my hold on her. I felt responsible for her safety and well-being

"Everything will be alright," I whispered in her ear, hoping that my words would provide some comfort amidst the uncertainty that surrounded us.

I watched as Sam very quietly said to Lily, "Whatever secrets you're keeping, they won't stay hidden for long, We can only protect you if we know what we're up against."

I felt a mixture of relief and apprehension as Lily nodded, accepting the gravity of the situation. She was willing to trust us, even if it meant exposing her own vulnerabilities.

"Would you like to come back to my place?" she offered hesitantly. "I can explain everything there if you don't mind."

Sam shook his head, his gaze fixed on the shadows that still lurked at the edge of our vision. "No, I'll stay here and wait for Miles and Henry. Rock, you go with Lily. Listen carefully and relay the information back to us."

"Alright," I agreed, "Let's go, Lily."

As we began to walk away from Sam, I couldn't help but replay Sam's words in my head. 'We can only protect you if we know what we're up against.' It was true – without understanding the threat that hounded her, how could we possibly keep her safe? And yet, as we moved further from the shore and deeper into the night, I couldn't shake the feeling that we were heading straight into the maw of some unseen danger.

I wrapped my arm protectively around Lily, pulling her close to shield her from her demons. My breath had started to mist in front of me while the distant sound of waves crashing against the dock walls filled the silence between our hurried footsteps. The tension from earlier still lingered, and I could feel it knotted in my gut.

"Here's my car," I said, clicking the key fob and unlocking the doors. As we reached the vehicle, I opened the passenger door for Lily and helped her inside. She gave me a small, grateful smile as she settled into the seat, and kicked the rubbish on the floor.

"Thanks, Matt," she whispered, her voice barely audible. I nodded, trying to offer her a reassuring smile before closing the door and walking around to the driver's side.

As I slid behind the wheel and started the engine, I couldn't help but steal glances at Lily. Her eyes were focused on the dashboard, but I could tell her thoughts were miles away. I wanted to reach over and take her hand, to tell her that everything would be okay once she shared her story with me. Yet, the fear that had been etched on her face earlier hung over my heart like an icy spectator, making it difficult for me to find the words.

The short drive to her apartment building was a quiet one, filled with the hum of the engine and the soft rustling of our clothing as we shifted in our seats. I could feel Lily's apprehension growing with each passing minute, and it took every ounce of my willpower not to reach over and envelop her in a comforting embrace.

When we pulled up outside the building, I parked the car and got out, opening the door for Lily once more. As she stepped out onto the sidewalk, her eyes flicked nervously around the dimly lit street, searching for any sign of the threat that had chased her earlier.

"Let's get you inside," I told her, gently guiding her towards the entrance of her apartment building. "You can tell me everything there, where it's safe and warm."

"Alright," she agreed, her voice barely more than a whisper. I could see the tremble in her hands as she fished her keys out of her pocket, and I knew that whatever secret she held close to her chest, was tearing her apart from the inside. And I couldn't help but wonder if, once she told me, it would do the same to me.

20

LILY JAMES

When we got to my apartment, Matt got me to sit on the lounge while he went and made me a cup of tea. My hands were still shaking, and I couldn't stop them, a mix of fear and adrenaline still running through my veins from this morning's events.

"Here," Matt said as he sat on the coffee table before me and handed me the cup.

"Thank you," I said, taking it and smiling at him with gratitude for his kindness and wanting to take care of me before anything else, as he grabbed the blanket from the back of the lounge and pulled it around my shoulders. His actions warmed my soul and made me feel even more connected to him.

I took a few sips of the tea, part of me trying to postpone all that I had to dredge up from my past and reveal to Matt and part of me just liked the fact that Matt was looking after me as I had been on my own for so long.

I had forgotten what it was like to have someone look after me this way. Matt just sat there next to me and patiently waited for me to be ready. While I knew he would never try to force it out of me, his Boss' words rang in my ears.

'Whatever secrets you're keeping, they won't stay hidden for long; We can only protect you if we know what we're up against.' I knew he was right, and I knew I could not hold off any longer. I put my cup down on the table and turned to Matt. He immediately took my hands, reassuring me that he was there for me no matter what. I took a deep breath in, closing my eyes for a second to gather my thoughts. Then I opened them, releasing the breath only to look into the most beautiful, loving eyes, the eyes of my "Mate" whatever that all meant and I hoped that that would not change once Matt knew the truth about my past.

"I'm not going anywhere, no matter what," Matt said as if reading my thoughts. His words caused a tear to run down my cheek. Matt reached out and wiped it away, stroking my cheek with his thumb.

"No matter what," he said to reassure me.

I nodded, and then I began.

"It all started just over a year ago; my family and I were invited to a fundraiser that was being held in Perth, My parents often got invited to these events, and I didn't usually attend, but this particular one, all family members were invited and my parents thought it would nice to attend as a family. We were seated at our table, and the night was going great, but then I noticed this guy staring at me. He smiled at me when I saw him and I gave him a curt smile back and returned to focus on my family, but I could sense he was still staring at me. I tried to ignore it; it just made me feel so uncomfortable." I took a breath and continued.

"After some time, he approached our table and introduced

himself; Dmitry Cosgrove was his name. He asked me to Dance, but I declined his invite; he was relentless, even asking my father's permission, but my Dad stated that if I didn't want to dance he wasn't going to force me. He didn't seem to take that response well; his anger was written all over his face. But he excused himself and returned to his table, but I could feel him staring at me the rest of the night; it got to the point where we decided to leave the event early." I revealed.

"I have no idea how, but somehow, he got his hands on my mobile number, and the next day, I started getting text messages from him. I didn't reply to them, but he kept sending them through. He asked me to go on dates, saying that he only wanted to get to know me, that he hadn't met anyone like me before, and that I was the most beautiful woman he had ever met." At this, I noticed Matt tense and his hands clenched into fists, but seeing me notice this, he released them and moved them between his legs out of sight.

"Go on," Matt said with a nod.

"He was obsessed with me right from the start. I confided in my parents, and my Dad found out who his parents were; they tried talking to them, but he had told them that I kept talking to him and I had been the one to pursue him. It all got so messy. My uncle is a Detective in Perth, and we spoke to him about it, but Dmitry had never threatened me or anything; he was just being a pest, and unfortunately, there was nothing they could do." I looked up into Matt's eyes and saw nothing but love there, so I continued.

"I changed my number, hoping that maybe he would just go away, but that seemed to worsen the situation. He got a hold of my new number and called me nonstop on private; I only answered once and never again, but the calls just kept coming day and night." I breathed and wrung my hands, knowing the worst part was coming.

"Then one night my parents had gone out, and I was home alone, a storm had hit, and the power was out, and I was sitting in the lounge room, when I heard a noise outside; when I got up to look outside I saw a figure just standing there in the rain, It was so dark, but I just knew it was him, I could feel it in ever fiber of my being. I grabbed my phone to call for help. But it rang, and without thinking, I answered it; it was him," I stated, looking up at Matt, looking for some reassurance to go on with the story, or maybe just some comfort to be able to go on. Matt reached out to me as if reading me and took both my hands in his.

"I'm right here," Matt said, looking at me with so much sincerity and care that I knew I could get through this with him by my side.

"I was met with heavy breathing and the sound of rain. I knew it was him. 'You will be mine; No one can keep us apart; you belong to me; I am your destiny.' He told me that I belonged to him and I didn't have a choice."

"That's why you reacted the way you did when I mentioned that we were just destiny," Matt said, understanding etched in his expression as he squeezed my hands.

"Yes, it just took me right back to that night," I said.

"What happened next," Matt asked.

I took a deep breath before continuing, thinking back to that night, which would forever be etched in my memory as one of the worst in my life.

"I hung up on him and tried to call the police, but before I could even dial the number, he was banging on my door, yelling that I let him in. His pounding was so hard I could hear the door splintering. I managed to call my uncle just as he broke through the door like something out of a horror movie; he walked in dripping wet and headed towards me. I took off running down the hall, trying to get away from him, but it was like he wasn't human; his movements were fast and double the length of mine, and before I knew it, he had a hold of me, picking me up off the ground like I weighed nothing and holding me against him. At first, I tried to fight to get free, but his grip was so tight it was almost crushing me, and the harder I tried, the worse the crushing feeling became," I said with shaking hands.

"I had no idea when I passed out, but when I woke up, I was in a dark room with only a single candle burning on the side table next to the bed. I have never been so afraid in my entire life, I didn't know where I was, how I got there or if I would ever see my family again, and it was terrifying." I admitted.

21

DETECTIVE MATTHEW ROCKLAN

With a careful hand, I guided Lily past the threshold of her apartment. The air was thick with unease—the kind that clung to your skin and made every hair stand on edge. I could feel the tension radiating from her in waves as we moved through the lounge, its familiar comfort marred by her palpable fear.

"Here, take a seat," I murmured, nudging her gently towards the couch. She sat, her hands wringing together, eyes darting around the room as if danger lurked in every shadow. I squeezed her shoulder reassuringly, hoping my touch grounded her in the here and now.

"I'll make you some tea." My voice might've been light, but my gut churned with trepidation.

The kitchen felt alien as I shuffled through her cupboards, the clinking of cups a jarring symphony against the silence. Finding the tea was like a scavenger hunt, with each cabinet a new puzzle to solve. But there wasn't any humour in it; not tonight. My fingers brushed against a box of chamomile. It promised calm. I hoped it could deliver.

"Keep it together, Matt," I muttered under my breath, the

steam from the kettle fogging up the window—a blurred view of reality. My heart banged against my ribs in anticipation, and each beat an echo of the fear I tried to crush down.

I couldn't afford to freak out. Not now. The thought of my wolf clawing its way to the surface sent a shiver down my spine. The beast within me stirred, drawn to her distress like a moth to flame. It would react to protect, to claim, to possess. But what would she see? A monster or a man?

"Control," I whispered, a mantra against the transformation.

I grasped the teacup handle—a lifeline to my humanity. It grounded me, the ceramic cool and smooth against my palm. The scent of chamomile filled the room, a hint of peace in a night fraught with shadows.

Can't let the wolf out. Not now, not in front of her, I thought, gripping the counter's edge until my knuckles turned white. Her story awaited—a tale I knew would test the limits of my restraint.

Stepping back into the lounge, the warmth of the teacup seeped into my hands, a small comfort against the icy knot in my gut. I extended it towards Lily, who sat huddled on the couch, her vulnerability palpable in the air that felt thick with unsaid words.

"Here," I offered, the simplicity of the gesture belying the complexity of my emotions.

"Thank you," she murmured, her fingers trembling as they wrapped around the ceramic. I reached for the throw blanket crumpled at the end of the sofa, draping it over her slender shoulders. Her running gear clung to her like a second skin, ill-suited for the chill that had nothing to do with temperature.

The steam from the tea rose between us, curling and twisting, an ethereal dance that seemed at odds with the tension that tethered us to the moment. I perched on the edge of the coffee table facing her, my own body coiled tight, every sense heightened. The scent of chamomile hung heavy, a feeble attempt to mask the scent of fear that clung to her like a shroud.

I watched—almost detached—as she fiddled with the cup in her hands. Her knuckles were white where they gripped the porcelain, mirroring my own internal struggle to keep the beast at bay. With each slow, deliberate breath she took, I willed myself to be the anchor she needed in the storm about to break.

She was about to dive into memories that clawed at her peace, and all I could offer was my presence. I wanted to wrap her in a cocoon and shield her from the phantoms of her past, but some battles had to be faced head-on, and this was hers. My role was to listen and support them, not to envelop her in a protective shroud that could suffocate them just as easily as it could safeguard them.

"I'm not going anywhere, no matter what you tell me." My throat felt tight and constricted as if my wolf was rising, pressing against my human facade, sensing the storm brewing within her.

A single tear broke free in the stillness, trailing down her cheek, carving a path through the day's grime. It shimmered, a beacon of her vulnerability; my hand reached out. My thumb brushed away the wetness, the contact brief but electric—a silent vow to wipe away all her tears if I could.

My hand lingered near her face, the heat from her skin a stark reminder of the life pulsing beneath it, a life threatened by shadows neither of us could fully comprehend yet. Retracting my hand, it returned to my lap, curling into a fist that I hoped could contain the restless energy surging beneath my skin.

Lily's voice broke through the silence of her apartment, each word heavier than the last. Her tale unfurled, a relentless cascade of fear and pursuit that had haunted her steps. My heartbeat throbbed in my ears, accelerating with the rhythm of her story. A stalker—someone who had shadowed her existence, turning every corner into a potential threat, every stranger into a potential enemy.

The room seemed to close in on me, the air growing thick. I could feel it—the beast within, agitated by her distress, pacing, yearning to break free and hunt down the source of her torment. But no, I wrestled with it internally, forcing it back. Not here. Not now. I couldn't risk losing control, not with Lily so vulnerable.

My fists clenched involuntarily, the knuckles whitening—a physical manifestation of the anger boiling inside me. An anger that wasn't entirely mine but belonged to the primal part of me that demanded action. A soft clink echoed as Lily set her mug down, and her eyes fell upon my balled hands.

I hastily, shifted my hands between my legs, out of sight.

Pulling the throw blanket tighter around her shoulders, and dove back into the narrative. With every revelation, my pulse quickened, fear for her well-being intertwining with the instinctual need to protect that scratched at my insides with sharp, demanding claws.

The room seemed to shrink with each word Lily uttered, the air growing thick, suffocating. I could smell the fear that clung to her like a second skin, acrid and pungent, and it mingled with my rising panic. Somewhere deep within, my wolf paced restlessly, its growls vibrating through my bones.

As she continued her tale, delving deeper into the darkness that had stalked her every step, my internal battle raged on. The wolf clawed at the edges of my consciousness, demanding freedom to protect, to hunt, to claim vengeance for the horrors inflicted upon our mate who'd come to mean more to me than I could ever have anticipated.

And we were only halfway through her story.

22

LILY JAMES

I could sense Matt's unease with the whole situation, it mirrored a lot of my own feelings, but my emotions were high on the fear of reliving the worst time of my life. Matt's was more an emotion of anger and vengeance, I had no idea how I could feel that from him, but I was certain that was the emotion he was riding on as I told him the details of my past.

I desperately wanted to stop, to not reveal any more of my past, but I knew it was time I stopped hiding from it and faced it head-on. I needed Matt and the others to know what they were up against, so that they could catch this monster and finally end the nightmare that had been my life for over a year now once and for all.

"The room was small, with just a bed and side table in it. Off to the right, there was a small bathroom with a shower, sink and toilet. There were no lights, just the one candle that I used to move through the room trying to work out if there was a way I could escape. I found the bedroom door but it was locked tight so I just went back to the bed and sat there waiting for what was to come next." I continued.

"I didn't have to wait long, maybe 30 minutes when I heard the bedroom door unlock. The light from the hall filled the room outlining the silhouette of the monster that had taken me and held me against my will. I said nothing as he stood there looking at me as if expecting me to speak first." I explained

"You're awake, were the first words he uttered as he moved into the room, his big form still blocking the door so I could not make a run for it. I just turned and faced the wall on the other side of the room giving him my back." I said while looking a the floor.

"It doesn't have to be like this, he told me when I ignored him, like I had a choice to be there. I continued to ignore him and I knew it was making him angry but I didn't care. I heard him click his fingers and a young girl appeared next to me placing a meal on the bed. Like I was going to eat something that he had given me. It could be poison for all I knew. Once the meal was delivered the girl exited and I heard the door shut and lock behind me." I paused for a moment before I continued, and took a deep breath as I knew the next part was going to be hard to get out.

"Days like this passed, each day he grew more frustrated that I wouldn't speak to him, and that I wouldn't eat. I wasn't even sure how much longer I could go without food, I was drinking water but only from the tap in the bathroom. I think it had been a week since he came into the room. He told me if I didn't start behaving that he would have to do something he really didn't want to do. He told me all he wanted was for me to get to know him without the outside world trying to influence me. He told me that he was trying to protect me. His words didn't even have any endearment behind them, they were harsh and sent a sense of fear running down my spine but

I never imagined what he was capable of," Matt leaned closer to me as I kept going, like he was giving me his strength.

"I started to eat the food as I knew I would need my strength back if I ever did get a chance to escape, but I still wouldn't talk to him, I just couldn't bring myself to do it. He started coming to my room and would lie on the bed for hours telling me about him and all these great things he had done and what we could accomplish together if I just gave him a chance." I explained.

"I couldn't help myself, I told him no matter how long he kept me there, no matter what he did, there would never be an us. Right away I knew I had done the wrong thing, his hands were around my neck so fast and he was choking me." I reached for my neck and rubbed it at the memory.

"He was so furious with me, I could see it in his eyes, his hands got tighter around my neck and I couldn't breathe, I clawed at his hands trying to get him to stop but he didn't, I thought that was the moment I was going to die. It all went black and I thought, it's over and I was at peace with it." I sighed.

"Clearly, I didn't die, he had just cut off my air supply long enough, that I had passed out. I woke up lying in bed and my neck was so sore it was hard to breathe or even move my neck. For a moment I thought maybe he had broken my neck but after a while, I was able to move a little more. I lay there for days, not being able to move. He didn't come to the room for days either, just the young girl who would bring me food and care for me, she never spoke but I spoke to her, telling her about me, about my family, trying to establish some sort of bond with her." I continued.

"After a few days, he came back to the room, he was all

apologetic, saying that he didn't mean what had happened. That I had just pushed him too far that day and that I should say sorry to him. I laughed, another mistake on my part but this time he didn't lay a hand on me, he just left muttering something about how he would make it so I would have to say sorry to him. He slammed the door so hard, I thought the door was going to fall off its hinges." I cringed at the reminder.

"Days passed again and I was beginning to go a little stir-crazy with only the light from the candle, and the space was feeling very confining. I still tried to talk to the girl who came in to bring me food but she either couldn't speak or wouldn't. She was still in the room when he barged in one day, 'Are you ready to say sorry to me' he asked with the most evil look in his eyes that kept me completely silent as if sensing something was gravely wrong. The next thing I knew his goons were bringing in 2 people with bags over their heads and making them kneel in front of the bed. I stood to attention knowing who they were instantly. Then lights flooded the room completely blinding me as my heart raced, I covered my eyes from the sting of the light and it took me some time for my eyes to adjust." I could already feel the tears running down my cheeks and I hadn't even gotten to the worst part, having to retell the horrific details of what I went through was becoming too much.

I am not sure when it happened but I was wrapped in Matt's arms and he was running his hand up and down my arms trying to comfort me. "Shh," I heard him say trying to soothe me, I looked up at him and he brushed the tears from my cheeks.

"We can take a break, okay?" Matt said, his eyes filled with genuine concern. Causing my heart to swell with gratitude. It was comforting to have someone show how much they cared for me, even though we were still getting to know each other. But I could also sense that he was struggling with the details of my story.

As much as I wanted to stop, just lay here in Matt's arms, just give us both a chance to gather our thoughts and comfort each other, I also knew that I just needed to get it all out and in the open so Matt knew it all, I was scared, scared of the past and the fact it was coming back to haunt me. Maybe finish the job, but mainly scared that after hearing all the details Matt would decide that I wasn't worth it. I knew deep down inside my soul, that if Matt could still accept me after knowing the darkest side of me, I could accept every aspect of who he was, wolf and all.

23

DETECTIVE MATTHEW ROCKLAN

I sit there, my heart pounding in my chest as Lily continues her horrific tale. The tension in the room has become almost unbearable, and I struggle to keep my wolf at bay. I can feel my nails lengthening, digging into my palms as I clench my fists.

Her words send shivers down my spine, and my mind races with images of her suffering. The darkness, the confinement, the fear - it's all too much. I can't help but reflect on how helpless she must have felt in that cold, dimly lit room.

I swallow hard, fighting the urge to wrap her in my arms and protect her from the world. But I know that's not what she needs right now. She needs someone to listen, understand her pain, and help her heal.

She shares more details about her captivity, each one more harrowing than the last. As she speaks, I can't help but marvel at her strength and her resilience in the face of such unspeakable horrors.

But even as I listen, fully absorbed in her story, I can't shake the nagging feeling that something inside me is about to snap. My wolf is restless, desperate to leap out and exact vengeance on those who harmed her. But I know I must keep myself in check, for her sake and my own.

As Lily's words weave their way through the dimly lit room, her fear hangs heavy in the air. I can practically taste it on my tongue, a bitter tang that sends shivers down my spine. My wolf stirs inside me, demanding to be set free so he can protect her from the unseen monsters of her past.

As she recounts the horrors inflicted upon her, I feel my control slipping away, bit by agonizing bit. My wolf snarls, desperate to tear apart anyone who dares threaten our mate. But there's no target for his fury, no enemy to sink his teeth into, only the weight of Lily's pain and the lingering echoes of her tormentors' laughter.

The weight of Lily's words hangs in the air, thick and suffocating. I watch as a single tear escapes her eye, trailing down her cheek before splashing onto her lap. It's like a dam breaking – suddenly, tears are cascading down her face in a relentless torrent.

"Hey…" I murmur, reaching out to brush them away. My fingers tremble against the softness of her skin, the warmth of it igniting something primal within me. Before I can stop myself, I'm pulling her into my arms, cradling her against my chest. Her scent is intoxicating, one that sets my wolf howling with the need to claim her right then and there. But this isn't the time.

"Shh," I soothe, rocking her gently back and forth. The growl in my throat is barely contained, a visceral reminder of the beast trying to claw its way free. "We can take a break, okay?"

As we sit there in the dim light of her living room, I close my eyes and inhale deeply, drawing in more of her scent. It's both a balm for the raging storm inside me and fuel to the fire threatening to consume me whole. I can feel the tension coiling in my muscles, the itch in my bones, the snarl echoing through the recesses of my mind.

"Matt?" Lily's voice cuts through the haze, her eyes wide and questioning as she peers up at me. "Are you okay?"

"Fine," I lie, forcing a smile onto my face, but my body is vibrating.

"Are you really alright, Matt?" Lily's voice was soft, barely audible over the roaring that filled my ears. Her eyes, those beautiful green pools, were wide with concern as they searched mine for answers.

I could have continued to lie, could have put on a brave face and told her everything was fine. But something in her gaze compelled me to be honest, to share the darkness that threatened to consume me. "Lily," I began, my voice cracking under the strain. "My wolf, he's...he's clawing his way out. He wants to hunt down people and kill them." I swallowed hard, feeling the weight of my confession settle like a stone in my stomach. "He wants to protect you, and I'm barely holding onto my control."

Her breath hitched, and her grip on my shirt tightened. I could see the fear flicker through her eyes, but it was quickly replaced by a steely determination. She needed to know the truth, and now she did. It was up to her to decide what would happen next.

My heart stuttered as Lily's eyes widened, the moss-green irises glowing with unexpected courage. She took a deep breath and said the words I never knew I needed to hear. "It's okay, Matt. He can come out if you need him to."

I stared at her, stunned by her willingness to accept the other part of me. But the thought of losing control around her sent a shiver down my spine. "Right now is not a good idea," I murmured, my voice heavy with emotion. "I'm not sure how he will react to you, Lily. He wants to claim you, sweetness. He wants to knot you, mark you, and own you. I can't allow that unless you want it."

Her gaze never wavered from mine, and I could see the determination flickering behind her eyes. As she spoke, my pulse quickened, the blood in my veins thrumming with a desperate intensity. "I do want that, Matt. I want to feel loved and cared for."

"Are you sure?" I asked, hating the vulnerability that seeped through my words. My hands trembled, sweat beading on my brow as I fought to keep my wolf at bay.

A small, reassuring smile graced her lips as she leaned in closer to me. Her fingers grazed against my arm in a gentle caress, sending shivers down my spine. "Yes, I'm sure," she whispered, her breath warm against my skin. My wolf calmed at the touch, his instincts telling him that this woman was our mate.

Without hesitation, she pressed her lips against mine in a soft kiss. At that moment, the world seemed to stand still as all of my worries and fears melted away. My arms instinctively wrapped around her waist, pulling her in close as desire coursed through my veins. I could feel my body responding to her proximity, my hardening dick straining against the fabric of my pants.

As much as I wanted to claim her right then and there, I needed to know the end of the tale first. Only then would I allow myself to fully give into our primal urges and make her mine completely. No one would ever touch or harm her again, she was my mate.

24

LILY JAMES

Kissing Matt was everything, I felt his love for me almost ooze into my veins. I felt his want for me straining through his pants. I desperately wanted to keep kissing him but now wasn't the time to get lost in each other, I needed to finish telling him what had happened to me no matter how hard it was to continue.

We both pulled back from our kiss and rested our foreheads on each other for a moment just catching our breath.

"My wolf needed that," Matt said, "You have calmed him a little," he added as I smiled at his words.

I pulled back from Matt and moved off his lap and sat on the lounge next to him, "What's his name," I asked making the assumption that Matt's wolf had his own identity.

"Matt," Matt told me with a smirk on his face.

"So no alter ego?" I asked shaking my head at him.

Matt laughed, "No, no alter ego, my wolf is just a more intense version of me," he said shaking his head slightly.

"I like it," I said with a slight smirk on my face, "at least I don't have to deal with learning another name," I added making him chuckle.

"Ha, Ha, your funny," Matt said poking me in the side as I laughed. We sat there for a moment just taking each other in.

"Is your wolf ok to continue?" I asked needing to know that I was not going to cause any harm to Matt or his wolf.

"Yes, we need to know the rest of the story," Matt told me his eyes flashing that golden colour I had seen before and I knew it was his wolf letting me know he was ok.

As we settled back into the couch, Matt pulled me into him. I rested my back against his chest, and he wrapped his arms around me. I instinctively rested my head against his shoulder, enjoying the comfort of being in his arms. I took a deep breath as I closed my eyes for a moment, gathering my thoughts and emotions, knowing I couldn't put this off any longer.

"When I opened my eyes, the cover over my parents' heads had been removed, and as their eyes opened, we all cried out for each other. I could see the fear in their eyes and knew they could see the same reflected in mine." I revealed.

"You are alive," My Dad cried to me, and I could see the relief flashing in his eyes.

"Of course, she is alive; she is my wife," Dmitry advised my parents and me at the same time.

"What?" I stated in complete shock and astonishment at the words that had just left his mouth. "I will never marry you," I yelled at him, "Look what you have done to me and my parents," I added, trying to get to my feet, but I was pushed back onto the bed by one of the goons he had with him.

"You will be my wife, whether you like it or not. You belong to me. I own you," he spat at me with such anger that I could see it in his eyes. He was going to make sure of it and that I didn't have a choice.

"I belong to no one," I spat back at him, my anger coming through without realizing it and not being about to stop myself. I knew he was trying to break me to try and take control of me, but I wasn't going to go down without a fight.

"He walked over to me and looked me deep in the eyes, both of us not backing down. I knew my resistance was getting to him; I could sense it, and just as I thought he would, he slapped me so hard across my face that it burned. The force made my face turn away from him, but as soon as it was gone, I turned back to face him, my anger written all over my face; I knew he saw that I was never going to back down and that he wasn't going to be able to break me the way he had others, so he did the one thing he knew would destroy me." I say, taking a breath.

"He smiled as he walked away from the bed, stood behind my parents and pulled out a knife. My heart stopped beating, and I held my breath; I knew what he would do even before the words left his mouth. I'll make it so you have nothing to live for," he stated with the most evil look.

"No!" I cried out, 'Please, no, I beg you,' I screamed at him, 'They didn't do anything to you!"

"No, you did, he spat at me, and now they will pay for your mistake." He told me back.

"I looked at my parents, and I saw the fear in my mother's eyes, but she was a fighter just like me; she raised her head high and told him, "My daughter will never break, not now, not ever, our love as a family will live on no matter what you do you piece of shit.' My beautiful mother was just as strong as she proclaimed I was." I said with a tear running down my cheek.

"And just like that, he slit her throat right there in front of me; I gasped, unable to say anything; I just sat there staring at her as he held her up, and the blood ran down her chest and onto the floor. He stood there staring at me and smiling like he was proud of his actions."

"I yelled at him, "YOU FUCKING ARSEHOLE, YOU THINK I WILL EVER LOVE YOU NOW, YOU THINK I WILL EVER GIVE YOU WHAT YOU WANT, I WILL NEVER BACK DOWN"

"He threw my mother's lifeless body onto the floor like she was garbage like she wasn't the most amazing, caring woman on this planet; he didn't care about what he had done. He just wanted me to suffer; he just wanted me to break," I say with a slight sob in my voice.

"'Really?" was all he said as he moved behind my Dad and held the knife against his throat. My dad said, "Look at me," and I did as he asked."

"No matter what happens, you survive," he said to me, and then all of a sudden, there was yelling and gunfire; it came from nowhere and was everywhere all at once. The goons in the room ran, and I jumped off the bed on the opposite side of the door to try and get some cover. Dmitry was shouting orders at his men, and that is when my Dad took the opportunity to fight back. My Dad was ex-army, so he knew how to handle himself; he was on his feet and ran at Dmitry like a linebacker, still with his hands tied behind his back." Seeing the event play out in my mind like it happened yesterday, Matt's arm held me tighter like he knew I needed the extra support.

"'Run, Lily," he called out to me as he pushed Dmitry

further from the door so that I could escape; I hesitated, not wanting to leave my Dad behind." I confessed.

"'Run Now!" my Dad yelled again as Dmitry started to get his footing, and with that, I took my chance and ran while I could. It broke my heart to leave my Dad behind, but if I stayed, all of it would have been for nothing. I heard Dmitry yelling for me to get back there and that he would find me no matter where I ran, but I kept running. Eventually, I found my way outside and across the courtyard. I saw my uncle and some of my Dad's ex-army friends." I explained.

"My Uncle spotted me almost immediately as I stood at the doorway while gunfire ran out in all directions. My Uncle ran towards me before I could summon the courage to move. The gunfire was so loud, and there was so much yelling. I moved towards him, but he put his hand up for me to stay, so I did. He wrapped me into his arms when he made it to me." I continued.

"You're ok?" he asked as he pulled away and checked me over."

"Yes, I'm okay," I said because physically I was, "but mum is…" I started, but the words caught in my throat.

"Dan," my Uncle asked, holding my sad gaze."

"I don't know, he made it so I could get out," I said as tears ran down my face."

"It's ok, but we need to move now," My Uncle told me as he used the radio on his shoulder to relay a message and then grabbed my hands, "Run and don't look back," he said, "No matter what, you get to that truck over there, that is your escape. You survive no matter what," he said repeating my Dad's words. I knew that they had risked their lives for me, and no matter what I did, I needed to survive."

"Ready?" my uncle asked me, pulling my attention back to him."

"Yes," I told him, nodding as if reassuring him that I was ready."

""Go!" he yelled at me, and I ran; I ran as fast as I could, focusing only on the van I needed to get to while shots rang out all around me. I felt a sting in my left shoulder, but I kept running; I needed to get to that van no matter what. It felt like forever, and my lungs and legs were burning, but somehow how I made it to the van. Two men who I knew worked with my father when he was in the army bundled me up and put me in the back." I explained.

""What about my Uncle?" I remember calling out as I tried to catch my breath, but they did as army men did. They focused on the mission, and saving me was their priority. We were screaming out of there in no time, stopping for no one and nothing, and I was left sitting there wondering if my Dad or my Uncle were alive."

25

I tightened my grip on Lily's trembling shoulders as we huddled together on the couch. The dim light only seemed to heighten the lingering shadows that clung to her face like remnants of a nightmare. I couldn't help but wonder how she had managed to carry on after such a tragedy.

"Lily," I asked softly, trying not to startle her. "How did you end up here, then?"

She glanced at me with tear-streaked cheeks and took a deep breath as if summoning the courage to relive her painful past. "After...after my parents died, my uncle was badly injured too. But my father's men managed to get me as far away as possible." Her voice cracked, but she pressed on. "The men he trusted drove me straight to Sydney and put me in a hotel."

I could see the pain in her eyes, the memories flooding back like torrential waves ready to drown her. It amazed me how she had managed to keep going despite everything that had happened. This girl was a fighter, and something told me she wasn't one to give up easily.

I sat there, taking in everything Lily had just told me. The room seemed to close in on us, the shadows of her past stretching across the walls. How did they manage to keep all this off the police reports? I couldn't help but wonder.

"How come your police reports are so clean? I mean, with everything that happened..."

She shifted slightly in my arms, her eyes downcast as she considered my question. "The men who brought me here told me that my uncle had me placed in witness protection," she admitted, her voice barely above a whisper. "All my records are fake, and my name isn't even Lily James. It's Lily Thompson."

"So," I began, "you never stole a car and went for a joy ride that ended up with you doing community service?" My voice was a mix of amusement and disbelief as I looked at her.

Lily laughed, the sound like music to my ears. "Nope, I've never even been booked for speeding," she admitted, her eyes sparkling with joy. It was almost like two regular people chatting for a second.

We both chuckled, the laughter easing the tension just a bit. I tightened my grip on her shoulders, trying to offer her comfort and support. "Is that it, then? Is there nothing else I should know about?"

Lily looked me straight in the eye, her expression solemn now. "That's it," she confirmed. "The rest, you already know. My nightmare is back, and he wants me."

A sudden, primal urge surged through me, and before I knew it, I let out a low growl. The sound rumbled deep in my chest, vibrating against Lily's back pressed to mine. Her body tensed momentarily, but then her shivering began – not from fear, but from something else entirely.

"Matt?" she asked hesitantly, her voice barely above a whisper. "What was that?"

"Sorry," I murmured, trying to suppress my wolf. "I didn't mean to—"

"Scare me?" she interrupted, a hint of a smile playing at the corners of her mouth. "You didn't."

Her scent filled my nostrils as I inhaled deeply, scenting her desire on my tongue; my growl made her wet.

"Does my growl turn you on, Lily?" I asked, smirking at her even as my own body betrayed my arousal.

"Um, maybe," she admitted, blushing furiously at the confession.

I reached out and grabbed Lily's hips, the warmth of her body radiating through my palms as I lifted her onto my lap. She was facing away from me, and I let my hands wander over her stomach before brushing my fingers teasingly against her top-covered nipples. Her body wiggled, and she moaned softly on my lap. The sounds she made sent shivers down my spine.

"Tell me to stop if you want me to," I whispered, my breath hot against her skin.

"No, please don't stop," she replied, desperation lacing her voice. "I need this. I need to forget for a bit."

With that, I gripped her hips once more, standing up and turning her body so she faced the couch. I pushed her back down with my hand, forcing her into a doggy-style position. My fingers hooked around her leggings and underwear, sliding them down her legs until they pooled at her ankles. I ran my hands over her exposed pussy, finding her dripping wet and ready for me. I felt a primal sense of satisfaction surge through me.

"Tell me to stop if you want me to stop," I said again, giving her one last chance to change her mind.

"Never," she gasped, and I didn't hesitate to push two fingers into her wet cunt.

Lily moaned and wriggled beneath me as I began to finger her. Her body responded to my touch, and I couldn't help but kneel and taste her. I growled as I licked and sucked at her clit, repeating "mine" over and over like a mantra. The sensation of her walls tightening around my fingers drove me wild, and when she came, her juices coated my hand.

As soon as she finished, I pulled my fingers out and licked them clean, savoring her taste. My pants were undone in an instant, my cock aching and dripping with precum as I gave myself a few slow strokes. Her pussy was on display for me, begging for me to claim it, and I couldn't resist talking dirty to her.

"I'm going to fill you up with my dick, and you're gonna love it," I whispered, smirking at the way she whimpered in response. Slowly, I pushed my cock inside her, feeling her walls tighten around me. She was wet, warm, and tight – everything I could've hoped for.

My thrusts started slow, but soon I found myself rubbing her clit in time with my movements, causing her walls to quiver around me. In one fluid motion, I leaned back up and hesitantly pushed a finger into her ass, asking if anyone had ever touched her there before.

"Never," she moaned breathlessly, and I felt a surge of possessiveness run through me.

"Good. You like that, don't you?" I asked, pushing my finger further in. When she confirmed that she did, something in me snapped, and I fucked her harder and faster. As I neared my climax, my fangs descended, itching to mark her as mine. My knot began to expand within her, but at the last moment, I pulled out and took a step back.

Her puzzled gaze met mine, and I covered my mouth with my hands, my eyes flashing yellow. "My wolf wants to knot and mark you, but you're not ready for that," I admitted, my voice strained.

Determined, she walked over to me and sank to her knees, taking my dick in her mouth in one swift motion. The sensation caused me to groan, and she pulled off, looking up at me with determination. "I'm still going to make you cum," she promised before sucking me hard and fast until I shot my cum, releasing my hot sticky load filling her mouth.

She pulled back, looked at me with swollen lips, then looked back at my dick, watching my knot swelling and licking her lips.

"What do I do about that? Want me to lick it?" she smirked at me.

My heart swelled with affection for her, and I couldn't help but smile down at her, fangs still bared. "I knew you were meant for me," I said, my voice thick with emotion.

Lily stood up and gave me a small, tender kiss over my fangs, her eyes shining with promise. "You can mark me next time, okay?"

26

LILY JAMES

I was on cloud nine after Matt left my apartment to go and update Sam on what I had told him. He said they would start to look for Dmitry using every available resource, but thinking about Dmitry and knowing all that he had already taken from me, that bubble soon burst, and I was back to reality. That reality was that Matt and the others could be hurt if they went after him or tried to stop him. I had already lost so much in my life, and I didn't want anyone else to get hurt because of me, but what was I going to do to stop it?

With a heavy sigh, I picked up the phone and called my Uncle. Dmitry had clearly found me, so now I could come out of hiding and contact the last living family I had. I dialed his number, which I knew off by heart but hadn't called once since I had left.

"Hello?" My uncle said as he answered on the first ring.

"He's found me," I spat out down the other end of the line.

"Lilly? How?" My uncle questioned with a heavy sigh.

"I have no idea, but he has, and he has been killing people

with no real rhyme or reason," I told my uncle, scared that the next time he was going to kill someone I loved.

"I'm coming; send me your address," my uncle convinced me, as if there was no way I would change his mind.

"You can't, please!" I told him, closing my eyes as my heart ached at the thought of him being the one who was killed.

"Lily, I need to," he replied.

"But you are all the family I have left," I told him, "I can not lose you, too," I added as tears ran down my cheeks.

My uncle was conflicted; I could tell by his delayed response; he sighed loudly before finally speaking.

"Lily, I love you, but like you, this animal took away everything from me; he took the lives of my brother and his beautiful wife, but he also took you away from me, too; even though you aren't dead, it was like you are, because I can't talk to you or see you, I just had to live with the knowledge that you were safe away from him. But now he is back and taking that away from me, too. I need to be there with you; I need to do everything in my power to protect you because that's my job now, do you understand?" He asked me as I took deep breaths to control my emotions.

"Yes," Was all I could get out.

"I will see you soon, baby girl," He told me before he hung up the phone. I fell to the ground, cradling my phone against my chest, wondering if I had done the right thing by telling him. Maybe I should have just dealt with this on my own because I didn't know if I could survive losing him; he was my only tie to my family left, and he meant the world to me.

My Uncle and my parents had saved my life that fateful day; they had devised a plan, knew the risks, and had done it anyway. I found out later that Dmitry had threatened them that if they decided to come after me, he would kill them and tell them that I belonged to him, and he would make sure that he was the only family I would have if they interfered. They knew eventually, he would come for them, and they swore they would save me no matter what.

I was alive because of their sacrifice, and my Uncle had risked his career to get me into witness protection so that I could somehow have a future away from that madman and his delusional thoughts. Everyone I had known in Perth thought I was dead that I had gotten caught in the crossfire and was shot several times, and I bled out on the way to the hospital.

I have no idea how he had done it, but everyone believed that I was buried along with my parents, and everyone had mourned the loss of our entire family, lost to an evil man, all because of his obsession with me. I will be forever grateful for my parents and their love for me, and I will never forget all that my Uncle had done for me. I owe them everything.

With these thoughts fuelling my determination, I decided I would do everything in my power to help put a stop to all this once and for all, and the first step was being able to control my fear for when I finally came face to face with the animal that destroyed my life and took everything from me.

I texted John, "Tomorrow I will take back my life once and for all," almost immediately, I got a reply: "See you in the morning, ready to work."

27

DETECTIVE MATTHEW ROCKLAN

The weight of my badge felt heavier against my chest as I stood outside Lily's house, my gaze lingering on the building. I could almost hear the quiet breaths she'd be taking inside, trying to stitch her world back together. The discomfort of leaving her side was a gnawing presence in my gut, but duty called with an iron voice. Four officers, all trained and ready, were the barrier between her and the world's darkness—two out front, their eyes sweeping the street with practiced vigilance, one lean figure planted firmly by her door, and another silhouetted against the glow of the main gate.

"Fuck," I muttered to myself, shaking off the unease like rain from my jacket, "keep it together."

My car keys jangled a metallic tune as I fished them out of my pocket, the sound cutting through the early evening's silence. I slid into the driver's seat of my car, the leather familiar and cold beneath me. Ignition. Engine humming to life. It was a ritual as much as a necessity; these moments, alone with the engine's growl, were when I became Detective

Matthew Rocklan, not just a man whose instincts screamed to protect his mate.

"Everything secure here?" I asked through the window to the officer closest to me, even though I knew the answer. Protocol and paranoia danced a tight waltz in my line of work.

"Locked down tight, Detective," came the crisp response, the officer's nod firm, his eyes never straying from their watch.

"Good." My reply was curt; the word clipped short by the fangs of worry that refused to release me. Those four officers were good at their jobs, the best even, but the beast within rumbled, questioning the wisdom of walls and locks against the kind of evil we faced.

As I drove, the city's pulse faded into a dull murmur, the distance from Lily's place stretching out like a protective moat. It wasn't far, yet each block seemed to pull me further from ease. Even with protection, the notion of her being alone gnawed at my insides, an itch beneath my skin that refused to be scratched. I mulled over her moving in with me, turning it around like a key, searching for its lock.

My car slid into the familiar darkness of the precinct's underground car park, the concrete tomb swallowing the last rays of daylight. I killed the engine, letting the silence seep in. The lift beckoned, and I obliged, ascending to the surface level where life buzzed and hummed with caffeinated energy.

The small coffee shop was a beacon of normalcy attached to the side of our fortress of law. With her apron dusted with grounds and the smell of roasted beans clinging to her hair, Katie greeted me with a beam that could've lit up the dimmest interrogation room. "The usual?" she chirped, her hand reaching out toward mine.

Instinctively, I recoiled, pulling back before flesh could

meet flesh. A low growl escaped my throat, rumbling from a place that wasn't entirely human. Her hand retreated as if burned, cheeks flushing with embarrassment. "Oh, sorry," she muttered, her smile now wilted.

"Katie," I began the apology on my tongue feeling like gravel.

"Matthew," she started, hesitance lacing her voice, "if I overstepped—"

"Sorry, Katie," I muttered, my voice flat and devoid of warmth. "But no more flirting, okay? I'm not interested in that way." Her hand had retreated from mine as if scorched by the frost in my words. She managed a faint nod, her smile dimming like the last ember of a dying fire.

"Sure thing, Matthew. Your usual, coming right up." She turned to prepare my order, shoulders hunched ever so slightly —a subtle wilt under the weight of rejection.

I tapped my bank card against the machine, the soft beep sounding too loud in the silence between us. The transaction was as impersonal as my demeanor, efficient and cold. I stepped aside, acutely aware of the physical and emotional space I'd put between us.

My gaze wandered over the neat rows of pastries behind the glass counter, their sugary scents a far cry from the musty tang of precinct paperwork and the sterile sting of antiseptic that awaited me upstairs. But even the comfort of familiar flavors failed to lift the pall that clung to me like a second skin.

Katie's movements were mechanical as she handed me the paper bag. Her eyes were downcast, starkly contrasting with the vibrant woman who used to banter easily. "Here you go," she said, her voice a whisper lost in the morning rush.

"Thanks," I replied, taking the bag without meeting her

eyes. I could feel the bite of guilt gnawing at my insides, sharp and unwelcome. It was a mess of my own making. Katie's flirtations had been a harmless dance I'd once indulged in, but now, in the wake of what I'd found—or rather, who I'd found—they seemed like betrayals I couldn't stomach.

Turning on my heel, I pushed through the door leading back to the lift, the paper bag crinkling in my grip. Though I wished to smooth things over, to offer some kind of balm for the awkwardness I'd inflicted, it felt impossible. My world had narrowed to a singular focus, and anything outside that tunnel vision felt extraneous.

As I strode away, the aroma of coffee and baked goods lingered a faint echo of normalcy in life, quickly shedding any pretense of the ordinary. With each step, I distanced myself from Katie, from the man I used to be—one who could share a laugh over a cup of Joe without feeling like he was cheating on his destiny.

There was a time for apologies and amends, but that time wasn't now. Not when every nerve in my body screamed for me to return to Lily, to cement the bond that had thrown my world off its axis. The wolf within paced restlessly, its impatience a low thrum beneath my skin, echoing my desires.

I mashed the lift button with more force than necessary. The doors slid open, revealing a vacant chamber that seemed to echo my emptiness. Each floor it halted at was an unwelcome interruption, the ding of its arrival grating against my nerves like nails on a chalkboard. I could feel the impatience of my wolf rising with every halt, its primal instincts clawing at the edge of my control.

"Easy, big guy," I murmured to myself, feeling the weight of the beast within as people filed in and out, oblivious to the turmoil under my skin. The sterile scent of the precinct mingled with the myriad perfumes and colognes of the day shift, but none of it could mask my kind's raw, earthy essence. It wasn't just being away from Lily that had me on edge—it was the vulnerability of being unbonded, the need for the anchor she'd become without even knowing it.

Once I reached my floor, I didn't bother with pleasantries or patience. The moment the lift doors parted, I was out, my stride purposeful and quick. The click of my shoes echoed through the corridor as I made a beeline for Sam's office.

"Yo, Henry! Miles!" I whistled sharply, not caring who turned their heads. "Meeting. Now."

Henry popped his head out from around a corner. His sandy hair was disheveled as always, looking like he'd just wrestled a suspect—or his own shadow. His goofball grin slipped into something more serious as he caught sight of my face. Miles appeared a second later, his expression grim and focused.

"Everything alright, Rock?" Henry's voice held a note of concern, but I wasn't about to unload on him in the hallway.

"Fill you in inside. Let's move." The words came out terse, clipped. Waiting for the elevator had been enough; my tolerance for delay was spent.

The door to Sam's office barely protested as I shouldered it open, the weight of my impatience making me careless with the niceties like knocking and waiting. A thrum of restlessness pulsed beneath my skin, an undercurrent that only heightened as I entered the dimly lit room. The air was thick with the scent of old leather and black coffee—a comforting blend that usually eased the edges of my wolfish irritability. Not today.

"Rocklan," Sam greeted without looking up from his

paperwork, voice steady as ever. I ignored the formality, striding across the room and collapsing into the chair opposite his desk. My hands were shaking faintly, a side effect of being too long in human form when the moon called for fur and fangs. I pulled the paper bag from my coat pocket and tore into the pastry, devouring it in three swift, almost savage bites. The coffee followed the liquid, scalding and bitter as it raced down my throat, mirroring the turmoil inside me.

Footsteps sounded outside, and the click of the door indicated Henry and Miles had arrived. The light shifted subtly as they closed the door behind them, and I could feel their eyes on me—sizing up my mood.

"Her real name is Lily Thompson," I said, leaving a sour tang of betrayal in my mouth. This piece of her past wasn't mine to share, but necessity was a cruel master.

Sam's hand stilled, and he lifted his gaze to meet mine. His fingers curled around the mouse, giving it a playful wiggle that seemed out of place in the moment's gravity. I watched as he typed the name into his computer, each keystroke a hammer blow to my frayed nerves. His eyebrows shot up, disappearing beneath the fringe of grey hair that fell across his forehead.

"Thompson, you say?" There was a note of disbelief in Sam's voice, a rarity for a man who'd seen the darkest alleys of humanity.

"Yep," I replied, letting the empty cup drop to the desk with a thud that echoed through the tense silence. My gaze remained locked with Sam's, the screen's glow painting his features in cold light. He didn't need to say it; I could practically hear the cogs turning in his head, pieces snapping together in a picture that spelled out trouble in bold, unmissable letters.

"Damn," he finally breathed, leaning back in his chair. The soft squeak of leather punctuated the confession of his shock.

Henry cleared his throat—a nervous habit that made him seem even more like an oversized, anxious pup than usual.

"Witness protection?" Sam's question hung heavy in the air, mingling with the faint hum of the precinct's fluorescent lights.

I nodded, a bitter taste lingering on my tongue. "Yeah. Dmitry Cosgrove stalked her, kidnapped her..." I paused, the images of that bloodied rescue searing behind my eyelids, "and when they finally got to her, it was too late for some. Her parents and a slew of cops never made it out." My voice was flat, but inside, rage churned like a storm. "Her uncle in Perth —a detective—he pulled some serious strings."

Henry's blue eyes widened, reflecting a shock that mirrored my own when I first heard Lily's story. Miles' jaw clenched, his anger obvious.

"So he found her, tracked her to Sydney, and continued his wrath," Sam concluded, his face hardening into stone.

"Let's hope he isn't supernatural, so we have the advantage against him," I growled, feeling the itch beneath my skin—the primal urge to hunt.

Miles shook his head, a grim determination in his eyes. "I don't think he is. I got a good whiff when we chased him down. Smelt human."

"Good," Sam said, his mouth twisting into a grim smile. "I think this one needs to be off the books. Jail isn't going to work for him. He needs to swim with the fish."

I couldn't help but agree, the image of justice being served in the darkest way settling an icy calm over my nerves.

"Assuming you're heading back now?" Sam's gaze bore into me, seeking confirmation.

"Can't be far from her," I admitted, shifting in my seat as the need to shift clawed at my insides. "My wolf is itching to get out..." But there was another pull, stronger than the call of the moon—Lily.

"Maybe you should shift in her presence?" Miles suggested, but the idea sent a bolt of fear straight through me.

"Can't," I said quickly, too quickly. "Don't trust myself."

"Right decision," Sam interjected firmly. "Bond then shift. Your wolf might be too scary unbonded."

"Totally agree," I muttered, pushing up from my chair. The floor felt cold and unwelcoming beneath my feet, mirroring the chill spreading through my chest at the thought of scaring her.

"Rock," Sam called out just as I reached the door, his voice laced with a leader's foresight. "Move her into your apartment. It's more secure, and it's more plausible if you kill him there instead of hers."

A savage grin spread across my face, my wolf resonating with the plan. "Oh, the fucker is dead. I'm gonna chew that heart right out of his body, eat it, then shit it out later," I vowed, the words tasting like a promise on my lips.

Henry's laughter bubbled up, a release of tension that shook his muscular frame. In contrast, Miles grimaced, his features pulling tight in distaste or maybe dread. Couldn't blame him; the path we were about to walk was stained in shadows.

28

I jumped as a knock came at the door and as if sensing my unease a voice called from the other side of the door. "It's me," Matt said instantly, calming me, as I walked to the door without a second thought and opened it.

There he stood, slightly dishevelled, as if he had been chasing down bad guys since he left me only a few hours ago. I couldn't help but reach for him, and he welcomed my embrace, pulling me into him so close that I snuggled my nose into the crease of his neck and breathed him in. I could feel him do the same to me. I was so captivated by the moment that I didn't even realize that Matt had lifted me and walked us into my apartment until I heard the door shut.

I looked up at him concerned that this whole situation too stressed him. "How did it go," I asked him as I lifted my hand to stroke his cheek. Matt buried his cheek into my palm closing his eyes for a split second before he opened them to answer my question.

"Everyone is up to date with everything, and Sam suggested that you move in with me," Matt said.

"What?" I asked, leaning back in his arms, shocked but not completely turned off by the idea.

"My place is more secure, I can protect you there, and if this piece of shit tries to come for you in my home, I have the resources to end him right there and then," Matt advised me, pulling me closer to him and closing the little distance I had put between us moments ago.

I looked up at Matt as the words he had just stated sank in. I knew he was right, but at the same time, moving in with him would put him in more danger in the end, and I couldn't have anyone else get hurt because of me.

"Matt," I started but he stopped me by putting his lips on mine and immediately distracting me as I began to kiss him back. I could sense his need for me just as much as I could feel my need for him. It was overwhelming how much I needed this man and wanted him to take me, to own me. I was completely at his mercy, and I didn't even seem to mind. Usually, I liked to be in control, a characteristic I had had since I was a child, but with Matt, it was as if all that went out the window, and I could give myself to him wholly.

Matt's kisses got even more intense as he lifted me off my feet, my legs instinctively wrapped around his waist, and he moved us to the nearest wall and placed me against it.

"I need you," Matt said as he broke our kiss.

"Then take me," I answered, my breath heavy and as I drew in a breath, a low growl came from the back of Matt's throat, sending a pulsing sensation deep within my core. I began grinding against the hard length hidden beneath his suit pants but well and truly straining to get out.

Matt moaned, his head falling back as he closed his eyes and moved his hips in rhythm with mine, a few second later his eyes were open and on me, the amber glowing in them as his wolf came to the forefront and a louder, more forceful growl came from Matt or more his wolf. I didn't take my eyes away from him, trying to show him that I trusted his wolf and wanted him to know I wasn't afraid. I leaned in and kissed him, our tongues lacing together, devouring each other. It was hot as hell, and I could feel the wetness between my legs building. As if sensing how turned on I was, Matt began moving his hand from my waist down the front of my shorts and didn't stop until he reached my pussy.

"So fucking wet for me," he moaned against my lips as he pushed two of his fingers into me.

"Oh fuck, Matt," I moaned as the pressure of his fingers entering me sent a bolt of pleasure to my core. Matt worked his magical fingers inside me while his thumb stroked my bud; the pleasure was both amazing and overwhelming all at the same time.

"I love your little moans," Matt whispered in my ear, "They are so fucking hot," he added as he nipped my ear lope.

"Make me moan louder," I taunted him, grinding down on his fingers and pushing him deeper inside of me, letting out a little gasp as the pressure rocked my body.

I wasn't usually this forward, but Matt had a way of making me feel safe enough to let go of all my fears. Just be who I wanted and needed to be with him. I knew I could tell him exactly what I wanted sexually, and he would accommodate my every need.

Matt gave a sly giggle as he began to work his fingers in and out of me, even adding an extra finger, earning himself a slightly more drawn-out moan from my lips as his thumb rubbed my bud. I could feel myself tightening around his fingers, and I knew I was close.

"Don't stop," I said, pleading with him.

"Come for me, Baby," Matt said, licking his lips, and it was as if those words called to me. Seconds later, I was coming, my juices covering his fingers and dripping down my thighs.

My whole body collapsed against Matt, my legs still wrapped around him as I panted against the crease of his neck, giving him little kisses. After a few seconds, I lifted my head and looked at him.

"You are amazing," I told him, looking him in the eyes.

"Funny, I was going to say the same thing to you," Matt stated, "You look so fucking hot when you come," he added with a smirk.

"Is that right?" I said in a sly tone; Matt nodded, his head tilted slightly to the right.

"How about you make me come again, then," I stated with a smirk on my face.

29

Lily was going to send me crazy; I just knew it. Her eyes, dark and sultry, bore into mine like they were searching for a hidden treasure within my soul. The room around us seemed to fade away as all I could focus on was her – the taste of her lips still lingering in my mouth, the scent of her arousal intoxicating my senses. My heart pounded in my chest, too fast and loud, drowning out any rational thought.

"How about you make me come again then," she whispered, her breath hot against my ear, sending shivers down my spine.

I stood there, holding her against the wall, her legs wrapped around my waist. My hand was still dripping with her juices, a testament to our earlier passionate encounter. I couldn't help but be amazed at how she had managed to take control of my entire being so effortlessly.

"Are you sure?" I asked hesitantly, trying not to let my desire betray the uncertainty gnawed at me.

Her response was a wicked smile, her eyes sparkling with

mischief and lust. "What's the matter, Matt?" she taunted, her voice low and sultry. Are you afraid you can't handle me?"

My heart pounded wildly in my chest, each beat echoing the primal urges that threatened to consume me. I could feel the heat of her body pressed against mine, warming me to my very heart. And yet, even as I drew in a shaky breath, it felt like all the air had been stolen from my lungs.

"Listen, Lily," I growled into her ear, my voice barely more than a whisper. "If I fuck you, I'm claiming you. You understand?"

She whimpered softly at my words, her body trembling ever so slightly beneath me. The scent of her arousal grew thicker, filling the air around us like an intoxicating perfume. It was clear that she wanted this – that she wanted me to claim her. And, God help me, I wanted it too.

"Please," she murmured, her eyes dark and full of need. "Do it, Matt."

My hands tightened on her hips, fingers digging into her soft flesh as I fought against the urge to give in to her completely. It would be so easy to lose myself in her, to let go of the last threads of control that kept me tethered to reality. But once I crossed that line, there would be no going back.

"Are you sure?" I asked, struggling to maintain some semblance of reason amidst the chaos of desire that threatened to engulf us both.

"Claim me, Matt," she urged, her voice both a plea and a command. And in the end, I could do nothing but obey.

My heart pounded in my chest like a wild animal trapped in a cage; the blood roared in my ears as I looked into her eyes. The room seemed to grow more suffocating by the second, and the heat between us felt like it was about to ignite the air.

"Which way is your bedroom?" I managed to ask, my voice barely above a whisper, raw with need.

"Th-that way," she stammered, her trembling finger pointing down the dimly lit hallway. Her breath came out in ragged gasps, her chest heaving with anticipation.

Gently, I started in that direction; her arms encircled my neck, drawing us closer together as if we were two pieces of a puzzle that had finally found their perfect fit.

"Matt, please," she murmured against my skin, her lips brushing against my throat as they sought purchase on anything that could anchor her in the storm that raged within her.

Every step brought us closer to the edge, to the point of no return, and I knew there would be no going back once we crossed it.

"Here," she whispered, her voice barely audible above the thrumming of my pulse.

Carrying her into the bedroom, I felt a shiver run down my spine as the cool air kissed our skin. The room was small and sparsely furnished, but it didn't matter – all that existed at this moment was us. Gently, I laid her out on the bed, her body sinking into the soft mattress. My hands trembled as they reached for the waistband of her shorts, hesitating for just a moment before pulling them down her legs with painstaking slowness.

"Matt," she breathed, her voice barely more than a sigh as her legs fell open, revealing herself to me like a delicate flower in full bloom.

"God, Lily, you're beautiful," I murmured, unable to tear my eyes away from the sight before me. At that moment, I knew I would do anything to keep her safe.

"Please," she whispered, her fingers tangling in the sheets as she arched her back ever so slightly, urging me closer. "I need you."

"Are you sure?" I asked, my heart pounding in my chest. The weight of what we were about to do bore down on me, threatening to crush me beneath its pressure - but one look into her eyes told me all I needed to know.

"Yes," she said, her voice steady and unwavering. Her eyes, wide and full of desire, seemed to beckon me closer. I couldn't resist her any longer. With a low growl in my throat, I leaned down and did exactly what she wanted me to, running my tongue from her ass to her clit. The taste of her exploded across my senses, filling my mouth with an indescribable sweetness.

"Matt, oh God," Lily moaned, her fingers gripping the sheets as her body arched towards me. "Don't stop."

"Trust me, sweetheart," I murmured against her heated skin, "I have no intention of stopping." I continued to greedily explore her, drinking in her essence and marking myself with her scent. Every sound she made only spurred me on, driving me to madness.

"Please," she whimpered, "I need more."

Pulling myself away from her, I could see the flush that had spread across her face, the swollen lips that begged for more attention. I pushed myself into a standing position, my hands fumbling with the button of my pants. My heart raced as the fabric slipped down my legs, pooling at my feet.

There I was, standing before Lily – my heart racing, desire pooling low in my gut. It felt like the world had narrowed down to this single moment. With a heavy exhale, I crawled back onto the bed, my cock standing at attention, anticipation and need evident in the pre-cum that glistened on the tip.

"Are you ready for this?" I asked her, my voice husky with emotion. Her eyes locked onto mine, filled with trust and passion. "I don't know if I can hold back this time, Lily. If we do this... it's going to be rough."

"Matt," she whispered, brushing her fingers against my cheek. "Shut up." She said with a smirk.

"Alright," I murmured, feeling a surge of possessiveness. Gently, I grabbed her hips, guiding her to flip onto her stomach and nudging her into position with her ass up and face down. My breath caught as I admired the view, all smooth skin and curves presented to me like the most decadent feasts.

"God, you're beautiful," I couldn't help but say, my gaze sweeping over the expanse of her back, the dip of her waist, and the swell of her hips. It was almost too much to bear, knowing that soon, I'd be claiming her as my own.

"Please," Lily gasped, sending shivers down my spine. "Claim me, Matt."

"Remember, sweetheart," I warned her one last time, my hand gripping the base of my shaft as I positioned myself at her entrance. "This is it. Once we cross this line, there's no going back."

"Matt," she repeated, urgency in her voice. "I'm ready. Please, just... make me yours."

"Alright," I breathed out, feeling the moment's weight settle upon me. With one final look at her, I drove myself into her smoothly, filling her. A gasp escaped her lips as I held myself still, letting her adjust to my size. It took all of my self-control not to move, not to give in to the primal urge surging within me.

"Matt," she whimpered, her fingers clutching at the sheets. "Please."

"Shh, sweetheart," I murmured, willing my body to remain still. "Just give it a second."

As the tension between us built, threatening to consume us both, I finally allowed myself to move, pulling back before thrusting forward in long, hard strokes. My focus narrowed to the sensation of her tight pussy enveloping me; our bodies joined together as one.

"Fuck," I groaned, unable to hold back any longer. The pressure inside me threatened to explode, a volcano of desire and possession that had been building for far too long.

"Harder," Lily begged, her voice barely audible above our ragged breathing.

"God, you have no idea how much I want this," I admitted, my words spilling forth unbidden. "How much I want to make you mine, forever."

The scent of our passion filled the air, a heady mix that threatened to consume me. I could feel the beast within me stirring, demanding to be unleashed. But I fought to maintain control, concentrating on the sensations coursing through my body and the woman beneath me.

"God, Lily," I panted, my voice strained with desire. "You're... incredible."

"More... please..." she whimpered.

Leaning forward, I grabbed a fistful of her hair, gently pulling it back to expose her neck. The sight of her pale skin, flushed with arousal, sent a shiver down my spine. I felt my fangs lengthen, the primal need to claim her growing stronger with each passing second.

"Are you sure?" I asked again, making sure she understood this was a forever thing.

"Y-yes," she breathed, and I could hear the trust in her voice. It was both comforting and terrifying.

"Fuck it," I muttered under my breath, deciding to take the plunge. Our bodies moved together in a dance older than time itself, the heat and friction between us building to an unbearable crescendo.

My legs grew stiff, and I knew what was coming next. The knot at the base of my cock began to swell, preparing to lock us together as I marked her once and for all. Gritting my teeth, I plunged deep within her, pushing past her tight entrance and forcing the knot inside.

"Matt!" she cried out, her eyes wide with surprise and pleasure.

"Shh, it's okay," I reassured her, biting down hard on her shoulder. The taste of her blood on my tongue only served to heighten my arousal, and I could feel her pussy spasming around me, drawing me in even deeper.

"Mine," I growled, the word barely recognizable as it left my lips.

"Yours," she agreed, her voice trembling with emotion. "Always."

The room seemed to vibrate around us, the intensity of our connection filling every inch of the space. With each heartbeat, I could feel myself becoming more and more a part of Lily as I emptied into her, my knot growing larger and securing our bond. The sound of her moans filled the air, a symphony of pleasure that sent shivers down my spine.

"Matt," she whispered, her voice raw with emotion. "I feel so damn full."

Her words pushed me over the edge, and I growled possessively, still latched onto her shoulder. We were one now, in every sense of the word. I could feel her thoughts, emotions, and soul entwined with mine.

As the moments passed, our breathing began to slow, and I could feel the knot inside her start to shrink. Carefully, I pulled back from her shoulder and licked away the blood that had seeped from my bite. I watched in awe as the marks on her skin healed before my eyes, leaving nothing but the mating mark – a testament to our eternal bond.

"See this?" I whispered, tracing the outline of the mark with my finger. "This means you're mine and only mine. No one can ever take you away from me."

A small smile spread across her lips as she looked up at me, her eyes shining with love and devotion. "I wouldn't want it any other way," she replied softly.

As I pulled out of her, I watched as my cum slowly dripped down her thigh, making that possessive side of me smile; I rolled myself down on the bed and pulled her on top of me, our hearts beating in perfect harmony.

"Thank you," I whispered, my voice barely audible even in the silent room.

"Always," she replied, her eyes never leaving mine as she reached out to pull me down for a tender kiss.

And with that simple word, I knew that no matter what challenges lay ahead, we would face them together as one. For we were bound by something stronger than love – we were bound by fate itself.

30

I smiled as I lay in Matt's arms while I gently traced the mating mark on my shoulder with my finger.

"It looks good on you," Matt whispered in my ear and kissed my forehead.

I looked up at him and smiled, "You think so?" I asked him and he gave me the sexiest smile in return.

"Yes, I think so," Matt confirmed as he used the arm wrapped around my back to pull me up his body so he could kiss me on the lips. His kisses always took my breath away and made me feel like I was the most desirable and loved.

When we pulled away from each other, my heart was racing, and my breath was ragged. We hadn't even been kissing for long, but that is what this man did to me. Now that we were mated, this is what he would do to me for the rest of our lives. That thought made me smile from ear to ear.

"What are you smiling at?" Matt asked me as he gazed into my eyes.

"Just thinking that we get to feel this feeling for the rest of our lives," I informed him.

"Oh, and what feeling is that," Matt asked, fishing for confirmation on what he already knew to be true. He pulled me even closer to his body as he awaited my answer.

"The one where I get to feel like the most loved woman in the world, where I know the one I love will always protect me with his everything and the feeling that life just could not get any better than this moment right now but also knowing that it can and it will," I told him, no holds barred, I wanted Matt to know how much I loved him and how being mated to him was the best thing to ever happen to me.

"I love you too, Lily," Matt told me as he leaned down and pecked my lips, "and my love will only grow deeper and deeper for you," he added, his lips just barely touching mine, his breath was warm, and he smelled like mint, How this man after everything we just did still smelled so good was beyond me, I most likely smelt like sweat and cum, not the best smell in the world. Still, I'd take it every time based on what just occurred. Matt kissed me again; this time, I was the one to move closer to him, and he let out a little moan.

"I could kiss you all day and night," Matt told me as he pulled away from our embrace, seeming to have something he wanted to say but was slightly resistant to.

"But?" I asked as I moved down his body, rested my hands on his chest and sat my chin on them, looking up at him, waiting for whatever it was he needed to get off his chest.

"Unfortunately, we have more pressing matters," Matt sighed as he ran a hand down his face.

"Dmitry?" I confirmed as my perfect little peace bubble popped and the reality of the situation came flooding back like a tidal wave. Matt must have sensed my unease as he pulled me back up his body.

"I won't let anything happen to you," Matt said reassuringly as he caressed my hair as my head rested against his shoulder.

"I know that Matt, but at the end of the day, you can't be with me 24 / 7, and Dmitry doesn't give up," I advised him more sternly than I intended as I pushed up off his shoulder and sat up.

Matt also sat up from his lying position and reached for my hand. "That's another thing I wanted to talk to you about properly," Matt admitted as he took my hand and looked into my eyes.

"I think you should move in with me," Matt spat out as if it was nothing, as if it was the easiest decision in the world, like what underwear he would wear for the day.

"Because Sam thinks it's a good idea?" I asked, still reeling from the statement. Was he just asking me because Sam said he should? Did I even want to move in with him? The idea definitely shocked me, and I wondered if he was asking for the right reason, but I wasn't completely turned off by it.

"No, not because Sam thinks it's a good idea, Because we are mated now," Matt stated, "That's pretty much married in my world, so we should move in together, right?" he added with a simple shoulder shrug.

He was right; I knew what I was getting myself into when I agreed to mate with him. But something deep down wasn't sitting right with me, and I needed to know.

"You didn't…" I began, but Matt cut me off as if knowing what I was going to say.

"No!" he exclaimed sternly, moving closer to me. I need you to look me in the eyes so you know I am telling you my whole truth," he added. I looked up at him, immediately feeling guilty that I'd even had the thought in the first place.

"I love you," he began, "You're my mate; we are destined. I want to protect you and come home to you every day," Matt said his honesty and truth boring into my soul as he took my face into his hands and pressed his forehead to mine.

"I'm sorry, it was a silly thought," I told him as my heart raced at his words and his touch, "I know you would never do that," I added knowing deep down I knew his truth.

"But..." Matt asked as if sensing there was more to my reaction.

I took a deep breath and gathered all my strength to tell him what was on my mind.

"I'm scared," I admitted.

"Of what?" Matt asked, looking at me with concern in his eyes.

"I still have nightmares about everything that happened to me and my family," I started as tears welled in my eyes, and I tried to hold them back. "The last people I lived with were my parents, and Dmitry took them from me for no reason other than he wanted me to suffer; he wanted me to have nothing worthwhile in my life to live for."

"Dmitry is an evil piece of shit that will pay for everything he did to you," Matt said, anger in his tone as his eyes darkened, and I knew his wolf wanted to come forward. I rubbed his arm, trying to calm his wolf with my reassuring touch.

"I'm scared it will happen again, Matt," I spat out, unable to hold back the tears this time. "I'm scared that he will see how happy I am with you, and he will do everything in his power to take you away from me. I can't deal with losing you, too," I finished as the tears started to stream down my face.

Matt moved closer to me, wrapped his arms around me and pulled me tight against him, his body against mine calming me slightly.

"Nothing is going to happen to me or anyone you care about, I swear to you," Matt said as he rested his chin on my head. "As long as we all stick together and have a plan to draw him out, we have the upper hand," Matt added.

He was right. We did have the upper hand. He had shifters on our side, and as long as we all stuck together, we could beat Dmitry and end this. The safest thing I could do would be to move in with Matt.

I nodded against Matt's chest and then lifted my head to look up at Matt.

"I'd love to move in with you, Matt," I told him with a smile. Matt gave me the biggest smile that extended all the way to his eyes. A quick flash of yellow appeared in them, and I knew his wolf was just as happy with my decision as Matt was.

31

DETECTIVE MATTHEW ROCKLAN

Today was supposed to be just another day at the office for Lily, but Sam had taken it upon himself to talk to her boss about getting some time off. It was some "official" police business, he told them. He was allowing her to take her holidays early.

I quickly glanced at my phone to double-check the details of the last-minute removalist company we had booked. They were scheduled to come to Lily's place in a few days to pack up her belongings and transport them across the city to my place. Moving in together was a major decision, but she was my Mate, and ultimately, she would have moved in with me regardless.

The sun was beginning to rise, casting a soft golden glow over the city as I told my credit card over the phone to the removalist company employee. "I'll pay the extra for you guys to pack it up and move it all," I said, rubbing the back of my neck. My wolf was growing restless, pacing inside me, eager for a run tonight.

"Sure thing, Mr. Rocklan," the employee replied. "We'll take care of everything."

After thanking the person on the phone, I ended the call. It was important for me to go for a run tonight; if I didn't, there was a chance that I would shift in front of Lily, and I wasn't ready to reveal that side of me to her just yet. Liam had agreed to come over and look after Lily while I went for my run.

I had asked Lily to pack a bag that would last a few days, just until the removalists could deliver her things to our apartment. The thought of it being "ours" was still foreign to me but in the best way possible. I never could have imagined being in this position, and now that I was, I couldn't imagine ever going back.

As Lily carefully folded her clothes into the suitcase, her movements were deliberate and unhurried. It was as if she were trying to savor every moment before fully committing to moving in with me. The tension between us was palpable, thick enough to cut with a knife. This was uncharted territory for both of us, and I didn't want to do anything to jeopardize what we had. As I watched her, a sense of excitement and nervousness mingled within me, knowing that we would soon start a new chapter together. This was more than just a physical move; it was a step towards building a life together, and I couldn't wait to see where this journey would take us.

"Hey, you need any help?" I asked, attempting to break the silence that had settled between us.

"No, I'm good," she replied, offering me a small smile. "Almost done, anyway."

"Alright." I tried to sound casual.

Lily zipped up her suitcase with a finality that made me

smile. As I wheeled it out to my car, I couldn't help but think about how much our lives were changing.

My nerves were getting the better of me when Lily climbed into the passenger seat. She raised an eyebrow at the mess of empty food containers littering the floor. "Wow, how did I not notice the state of your car the other night? You live like this?"

"Hey, cut me some slack," I defended myself, trying to laugh it off. "I'm always on the job. Honestly, I can't remember the last time I had the car cleaned."

She laughed, placing her feet gingerly on top of the debris. "I can see that."

"Sorry," I said sheepishly, feeling foolish for not keeping my car clean. In my line of work, there never seemed to be enough time for anything, let alone tidying up.

The city landscape danced in Lily's eyes as we cruised smoothly toward my apartment. Traffic was mercifully light, and the closer we got to our destination, the more settled I felt. My wolf's restlessness eased, sensing that our mate would soon be safe within our den.

"Almost there," I murmured, reassuringly squeezing her hand. She smiled at me, her gaze warm and trusting. I hoped she knew just how much she meant to me.

I pulled up in my regular spot on the sidewalk, quickly hopping out of the car to open the door for Lily. The cool air caressed my skin as I rounded the back of the car to grab her suitcase from the trunk. "Ready?" I asked, looking over at her.

She nodded a determined sparkle in her eyes. "Ready."

"Alright, then." I locked my car and led her up to my unit, my heart pounding with anticipation. As we walked, I couldn't help but feel a pang of insecurity. If Lily thought my car was a mess, what would she think of my apartment? I racked my brain, remembering if I'd cleaned it recently. But, as with my car, I came up blank. I could only hope it wasn't as bad as I feared.

"Is everything okay?" Lily asked, her voice soft with concern. She must have sensed my unease.

"Uh, yeah," I replied, forcing a smile. "Just... you know... wondering when I last cleaned the place."

"Matt," she said gently, squeezing my hand. "I'll train you.." she smirked at me.

I laughed at her as I headed towards the stairs, eager to get this over with, when Lily stopped at the elevator. She raised her eyebrows at me, a playful challenge in her eyes. I couldn't help but grin and change course, joining her by the elevator like the good boy that I was.

"Can't resist a shortcut, huh?" I teased, pressing the call button for the elevator.

"Hey, it's not every day you move into your boyfriend's place," she replied with a smirk.

The thought made me chuckle, and Lily caught my eye, curious. "What's so funny?"

"Nothing much," I said, leaning against the elevator wall as we waited. "Just thinking about what a good boy I am, waiting here with you instead of taking the stairs."

Her laughter rang out, echoing through the hallway. "Oh, I'm sure you're not always such a good boy," she retorted, playfully nudging me with her elbow.

"Are you implying something?" I feigned offense, raising an eyebrow. The elevator doors slid open, and we stepped inside and listened to the music that set that perfect elevator atmosphere as it rose to our apartment.

The elevator dinged, its doors sliding open with a whisper.

We stepped onto my floor, the dim hallway lights casting shadows on the walls, giving them an eerie, melancholy quality. Lily's curiosity and excitement bubbled beneath the surface as we approached my apartment door.

"Here we are," I said, fumbling with the keys before unlocking the door. Just as Lily crossed the threshold, I scooped her into my arms, catching her off guard. Her startled laughter filled the air as I carried her inside, setting her down gently on the cool kitchen tiles.

"What the fuck was that?" she asked, hands on her hips and amusement dancing in her eyes.

"What? You're supposed to carry the bride into the house, right?" I couldn't help but smirk at her reaction.

"Excuse me, I didn't bloody marry you!" She feigned indignation, but there was a twinkle in her eye that gave her away.

I walked back up to her and leaning in close, I lightly bit her claiming mark. "No, you did something even better," I whispered. "You became my mate." Lily's cheeks flushed, but she held my gaze.

"Hey, do you want a tour of the place?" I asked Lily, as she surveyed our new shared living space with a critical eye.

"Actually, I think I'd rather have some cleaning products so I can move my way from room to room myself," she said, wrinkling her nose at me. I laughed, knowing that she was probably right about the state of my apartment. "It's not that bad! I do have it cleaned. But yes, you're probably correct – I was a single male, working 24/7. Cleaning wasn't high on my list."

"Clearly," she teased, and I couldn't help but grin at her playfulness.

I walked into the kitchen and opened the cupboards under the sink, pulling out an assortment of cleaning products. "Since I'm off for the foreseeable future, how about we go through this place together? We can get rid of whatever furniture you don't like along the way."

Lily smiled, warming my heart with a simple gesture. "I love that you're making room for me in here, and not just squeezing me into your life."

My chest swelled with pride, and I scooped her up again, carrying her towards our – now shared – bedroom. "Baby, you're my whole life. I won't just make room; I'll let you take over the whole thing. You're my queen, and I'm happy to just play the Joker in this tale."

Her laughter filled the room as I leaned down to kiss her thoroughly. I placed her feet back on the floor and turned her to face the room. "Now this is our room. The only thing you need to keep is the blinds; the rest, I really don't give a shit about." I tell her.

32

LILY JAMES

It still seemed so unreal to me that I was living with Matt, we honestly didn't know that much about each other really, but I looked forward to finding out his little quirks. But for now, I would have to put that all aside, my Uncle had landed and I was meeting him at John's studio. The studio was a safe location that Matt had agreed on after going back and forth with Sam on the best possible location. We had to make sure my Uncle wasn't being followed.

As Matt and I drove to John's studio I felt off, it had been years since I had seen my Uncle and I knew it was going to be bittersweet because my parents were no longer here, but I could not shake the unease I felt as we drew closer. I tried to push it out of my mind and put it down to the fact that maybe I was just nervous, even before I had to disappear I hadn't spent much time with my Uncle. He was always under cover or working long hours so it was only really special events that we crossed paths.

He was always the fun Uncle when he was around that part I do remember, like he was making up for lost time. As we pulled into the car park my stomach was in knots. Matt parked and turned off the engine and turned to me taking my hand.

"Are you ok?" he asked me, concern etched across his face as his thumb rubbed back and forth on the back of my hand as he tried to comfort me.

"Yes, I'm fine," I said quickly giving Matt a reassuring smile as he looked at me unconvinced. "Just nervous to see my uncle I guess?" I added trying to offer some answer for my unease to both of us.

"Ok," he said, nodding and releasing my hand so we could both exit the car. Matt walked around to my side of the car and took my hand, as we walked together to the entrance of the studio. It was quiet inside which was odd for this time of the day and I could sense Matt tense as he went into high alert. We continued into the studio, Matt going in first as I flanked him from behind, my unease so strong that my hands were beginning to sweat.

"Which way is John's office," Matt asked me, pulling me closer to his side as he looked around the empty studio.

"Through the workout room, there to the right," I answered Matt, nodding towards John's office.

"Stay close," Matt muttered to me as we moved towards the office, he then reached into his pocket and pulled out his phone, hitting 1 and then the green phone button as he brought the phone up to his ear. I knew he was calling his Alpha Sam.

"What's up Rock?" Sam said as he answered.

"Just arrived at John's studio, it's all quiet here," Matt advised making me curious as to why he had called Sam, was he meant to be calling in to check up?

I could barely make out what Sam said, but I could have sworn he said, "On our way, don't do anything stupid," but surely I had misheard. Maybe I wasn't the only one that was feeling the unease of the situation.

"No worries will call if anything changes," Matt answered and hung up the phone putting it back in his pocket, just as he did the door behind us slammed shut startling me as I jumped from the sound. Matt swiftly moved to put himself between me and whoever had come through that door.

"Lily?" a voice called and I knew it was my Uncle. When I looked I also saw that my Uncle was with someone, as they both walked further into the studio I realised the man my Uncle was with was the very person that my Uncle had sworn revenge on.

I blinked as I tried taking in the scene before me. My Uncle the man who had saved me from Dmitry was now standing alongside him. I had not even noticed that Matt had backed us up further into the studio trying to keep some distance between them and us, our only advantage at this point. My heart was racing and I could sense my breathing was becoming more rapid and the room was beginning to get darker.

"Breath Lily," Matt whispered into my ear bringing my attention back to the room and the situation at hand, I needed to get my breathing and emotions under control if I was going to help get us out of this situation.

"What's wrong Lily?" Dmitry asked, "Not happy to see me?" he added with an evil laugh.

It was as if his laugh ignited a fire in me, I glared at him squaring my shoulders and standing tall.

"What the fuck is going on here?" I demanded as I glared at both Dmitry and my Uncle.

My Uncle laughed, "There's that firecracker I am used to," he stated taking a step closer.

"That's close enough thanks," Matt stated stopping him in his tracks as if only just noticing he was in the room, he eyed Matt up and down.

"What…? I mean no harm," my Uncle stated, "Just an Uncle reuniting with his long-lost niece," He sneered at Matt.

"Maybe I'd believe that if you weren't standing next to the evil fuck who kidnapped her and kept her against her will," Matt snapped.

"He didn't hurt her did he?" My Uncle stated so non-shelont that what Dmitry had done was nothing. Something was going on and I was over wondering.

"Are you going to tell me what the fuck you are doing, with the evil fuck who kidnapped me and killed my parents, your brother and sister-in-law, your only family…" I barked at my uncle as the anger boiled within me.

"Oh, Lily… Lily… Lily…" my Uncle said shaking his head, "You just don't get it do you?"

"Then explain it to her," Matt said calmly against my side as if unphased by the whole situation while I was about to lose my mind.

"Dmitry here, only did what I asked him to do," my Uncle stated shrugging his shoulders as I looked at Dmitry who was grinning from ear to ear like a Cheshire cat, as if he was proud to be someone else's puppet.

So many thoughts were running through my head, why would my Uncle do this to me and then like a slap to the face, the realisation hit.

"You had your own brother and his wife killed!" I stated, glaring at him in anger and disgust, he looked at me and said nothing. His face was unreadable for a moment as if the words

I had spoken hadn't even registered, and then he smirked at me amused by my pain.

"Why?" I yelled at him, the anger boiling deep in my soul at this man. I believed he had helped save my life for all these years when he was actually the one who had caused all my heartache and pain.

"Because I fucking hated him," he spat back at me, "The perfect fucking son… with his perfect wife and child… living this amazing life. The life I was meant to live," he yelled, his face turning red. "And you want to know the best part? He wasn't even my biological brother; that fucking cunt was adopted, and still I was treated like the leper of the family, cast aside and made to feel like I was worthless!"

"So this is all because your mummy and daddy didn't love you enough," Matt stated as my Uncle turned to him with rage still etched all over his face.

"This is all because he stole my life," my Uncle seethed through gritted teeth, "And when I held my gun to his head and he asked me why, I told him exactly that," he smiled at the memory, "Then I went into great detail about how I would torture his child for the rest of her life and he would not be there to protect her and then I shot him in the head," he said with a shrug like it was nothing.

"No!" I cried not believing that my father had died at the hands of someone he trusted.

"I should have known that fucker was already onto me," my Uncle continued, "He had arranged his own team to get you out safely and take you away, to a place not even I knew the destination of and none of his Army friend's were giving up your location, even after being tortured for hours," he said with a look of disgust on his face like he had been greatly inconvenienced.

I closed my eyes his words sinking in, all this time I had thought my uncle was a part of keeping me safe but my Dad had been the one to work out that my Uncle was not the person he made himself out to be and he had planned my safe escape and protection. He and his Army friends had been killed for it. More people had died because of me and I hadn't even known.

"Their deaths are not on you," Matt whispered in my ear knowing exactly where my thoughts had gone through our bond link, "He is an evil fucker who will pay for his crimes," Matt stated squeezing my shoulder.

"So Dmitry was just your puppet?" Matt asked his head cocked to the side like he was assessing the situation.

"There you go, you are starting to get it," he smirked back at Matt. Dmitry looked towards him and then back to us, "In fact now that I have found you, I don't even need him anymore," my Uncle stated as he raised a gun I didn't even know he had in his hand and shot Dmitry in the head.

I screamed, the shock of the situation startling and scaring me so much that I began to shake, Matt pulled me behind him as my Uncle then turned the gun towards us.

"It's time you come with me, Lily darling," my Uncle said.

"That is not fucking happening," Matt growled at him.

"Did you just growl at me?" my Uncle stated staring at Matt with what looked to be rage and curiosity. "She belongs to me," he added as if knowing those words would antagonise Matt and it worked.

Matt's anger radiated off of him in a deep, guttural growl as his entire body tensed and his fingernails dug into my skin as he pulled me protectively behind him.

I cried out at the force causing Matt to look down at me and assess the situation. Almost immediately his shift stopped, his nails retreated and the hairs that had started to stand up on his skin softened again.

Just as Matt was returning to his full human state, the doors to the studio flew open and in stormed Sam and the other detectives.

"Where is he," Sam called out to Matt, but when we turned to look in the direction where my Uncle had been standing he was nowhere to be seen. Like he had vanished into thin air.

33

DETECTIVE MATTHEW ROCKLAN

I couldn't believe it - the bastard had vanished into thin air. One moment he was right there, and the next... poof! Gone. Fuckwit. I glanced over at Sam, who looked just as bewildered as I felt.

"Quickly, change and follow the scent," Sam barked at Liam and Luke, desperation lacing his voice.

Without hesitation, they started stripping down right then and there. Their clothes fell to the floor, revealing their muscular bodies. There was a tense energy in the air, punctuated by cracking bones and the shifting of flesh as they transformed into their wolf forms.

I turned my gaze to Lily, whose eyes were so wide they looked like they might pop out of her head. Her mouth hung open, and she stared at the scene in shock. With a smirk, I whispered, "You're catching flies, love."

"Wha-" she stammered, snapping her mouth shut and looking at me with an expression that seemed to scream, 'Is this happening?'

"They... their wolves?" she stammered, her voice barely more than a whisper.

I couldn't help but laugh, even though the situation was far from funny. "Well, yeah, you did know this," I reminded her gently. "But seeing it and believing it is two different things, huh?"

"It's just... surreal," she admitted, shaking her head slowly as if trying to clear her thoughts.

I Leaned in to press a gentle kiss against her forehead. "Are you okay, sweetness?"

She shook her head, tears glistening in her eyes. "Honestly? No. My uncle... and now wolves... I need a nap." She rubbed her temples, looking utterly overwhelmed by everything that had happened in such a short amount of time.

"I know it's a lot to take in," I told her softly, wrapping my arm around her for comfort.

"Matt," Sam's voice brought me back to the present. "They said the scent is gone?"

I frowned, feeling a knot tighten in my stomach. "What do you mean 'gone'?" I asked, trying to keep the edge out of my voice.

"Like it led outside and now it's just... vanished," Sam explained, his eyes searching the area around us. "But they smell fresh blood. They're following that trail instead."

"Shit," I muttered under my breath.

I felt Lily's panicked grip on my t-shirt. Her voice was shaking as she realised what we were all dreading: "Where is John?"

My heart clenched in a vice-like grip, and I knew this wasn't going to end well. I shot a desperate glance at Sam, who seemed just as concerned. "Shit... where are Liam and Luke?" I asked, feeling my own panic rising.

"Shit, this way," Sam muttered, taking off around the back of the building with me and Lily close behind. Our footsteps echoed on the pavement, heavy with dread.

As we rounded the corner, the grisly scene unfolded before us: John sprawled on the cold cement, blood staining his clothes and pooling around him. Liam and Luke stood over him in their wolf forms, ears flattened against their heads and tails hanging low.

"God, no..." I breathed out, staring at the lifeless body of Lily's friend. I could see Lily's face crumple in anguish, her hand flying to her mouth in horror. She trembled like a leaf in the wind, her eyes wide and unseeing.

Lily's piercing scream shattered the tense silence that had settled over the grisly scene. I could feel her fear and despair like a tangible force, clawing at my chest as I pulled her into my arms. The sight of John's lifeless body was burned into my memory; his throat slashed from ear to ear, blood staining the cold cement beneath him.

"John was a trained fighter! How is he dead? This isn't right!" Lily sobbed into my shoulder, her voice raw and choked.

"Shh... I know, I know," I murmured, trying to comfort her as we moved away from the crime scene. Liam and Luke, still in their wolf forms, watched us with haunted eyes.

"Matt, this can't be happening..." she whispered against my neck, her body trembling violently in my embrace.

I had managed to bundle Lily into my car and get her home not long after Sam had called the crime scene in. My hands were shaking on the steering wheel, gripping it tightly as I tried to make sense of everything that was happening. We had planned to keep it off the books, but with this new revelation, we were now certain we needed the help.

"Matt, what's going to happen?" Lily asked, her voice trembling as she clutched at the door handle, her knuckles turning white.

"Hey, don't worry," I reassured her, although I wasn't sure if I believed it myself. "We've got some friends who can help us out. They're part of the local police force and SWAT team—shifters like us."

"Shifters? On the SWAT teams as well?" She looked at me incredulously, her eyes widening in surprise.

"Yup, where everywhere Sweetness. Trust me, they'll be able to help us." I tried to sound more confident than I felt.

"Okay." Her grip on the door handle relaxed slightly, and she leaned back against the seat, staring out the window. I let out a small sigh, feeling the weight of responsibility falling heavily upon my shoulders.

In a flurry of urgency, Sam called for an assembly of shifters at his residence. He purposely excluded me from the meeting, knowing I needed to stay by Lily's side till this was all dealt with. Sam needed assistance - someone skilled in tracking and surveillance. Our mission was to keep Lily safe, as her uncle's military background gave him an advantage. But he was not familiar with the world of shifters and their unique abilities that we could harness and use to our advantage. We needed a team of skilled trackers who could stand watch outside our apartment, ready to pounce at any sign of danger.

The world outside had started to fade into darkness, the only light in our apartment coming from the dim glow of a lamp in the corner. Shadows danced across the walls, mirroring the tension that hung heavy in the air.

"Sam contacted the police in Perth," I told Lily softly, trying to reassure her. "He's arranged for forensics to look into everything. They're searching your uncle's house right now."

"Good," she murmured, her voice barely audible. She was still staring off into space, lost in her thoughts.

I settled onto the couch behind her, wrapping my arms around her and pulling her close, like a koala clinging to a eucalyptus tree. My body heat seemed to seep into her, and I felt her tense muscles slowly begin to relax. "It's going to be okay, Lily. We've got this."

She leaned back into my embrace, taking a shaky breath. "I know you'll do everything you can, Matt. I just... I never thought it would come to this."

Before either of us could say anything else, the front door of our apartment was suddenly kicked in with a deafening crash. A split second later, the room was filled with tear gas, burning my eyes and throat as I struggled to breathe.

"Matt!" Lily gasped, her fingers clawing at my arms as panic surged through her.

"Stay low," I choked out, forcing my body to move despite the pain. "Hold your breath, and follow me. We need to get out of here, now!" But just as I said it, a pain spread across my leg, and I ran my hand down and found a small, slender metal thing sticking out of it; I pulled it out and held it up, and fear flooded my system; it was a tranquillizer. Fuck… was all I could think as my vision turned black.

34

"Matt!" I called out to him as my eyes burned, but he didn't respond. "Matt!" I yelled out again, using my hands to try to find him. I closed my eyes, trying to stop the burning that was causing them to water.

"Grab them," I heard voices say as I tried to open my eyes, but the pain was just too extreme. Heavy hands grabbed at my arms, hauling me up off the ground.

"Let me go," I screamed as I lashed out at the person, kicking and trying to pull away from their grasp.

"Stop moving, or I'll tranquillise you too," the goon replied in a gruff tone. Relief washed over me at the realization that Matt was okay. He had just been tranquillised and while not an ideal situation, knowing that he was okay calmed me slightly.

"Get them, let's go," another voice called from over near the door. I didn't recognise any of the voices, but why would I? It was most likely some goons my Uncle had hired.

The guy holding my arm turned me towards the door and pulled me along next to him as we exited the apartment. I turned behind me and slightly opened my eyes to see if Matt was ok. Two men had him, one on each side of him, holding him up by his arms and dragging his feet along the ground.

My arm was yanked, pulling my attention back to the man who was dragging me, "Eyes ahead," he barked at me as I glared at him with a snarl; my eyes had started to feel better, allowing me to open them fully. We moved quickly down the hall and then to the stairs and moved quickly down them, too. I could hear Matt's boots hitting each step as they descended, and I was glad that we hadn't even had time to take our shoes off when we got home, as at least his feet were protected.

"Where are you taking us?" I asked as we reached the bottom of the stairs, pulling my arm back from the man who was holding me, but he didn't let go or loosen his grip.

"You will find out when we get there," he answered with a wicked chuckle that made the hairs on the back of my neck stand to attention.

When we reached the bottom level, a van was waiting right at the gate. It was parked up on the sidewalk, and I noticed on the side of the van that it had a council logo, clearly stolen. It looked like it was meant to be here and didn't draw any attention. The side door was open already, and I was dragged into the van, still being pulled along by old mate and his harsh grip.

"Sit," He said, pushing me down to the ground and I fell with a thud, my butt hitting the metal floor hard. My head hitting the side of the van causing me to wince at the shock and slight pain that followed. Matt was then dragged into the van by the two men and he was pretty much tossed onto the floor as they dumped him and exited, and the door was forced shut with a loud thud.

"Matt," I called out as I moved over to his side and rolled him over onto his back. I could see his chest rising and falling, and I blew out a breath I didn't even realize I was holding. It was one thing thinking Matt was alive, but actually confirming it calmed my soul.

"You're ok," I said out loud, not really sure if I was trying to convince myself or tell an unconscious Matt he was ok. I pushed his hair back off his face, and he felt like he was on fire; he always ran hot, but this was beyond his normal temperature; it was like he had a fever; then I noticed the beads of sweat on his forehead as I heard a slight growl sound low in his chest. I put my hand on his chest so that he knew I was there and to calm him.

Moments later, the front doors of the van opened, and the three men climbed inside, one looking back to check on us.

"Good to go?" The one in the driver's seat asked.

"Yeah, he's out cold and should be for hours," the one who had looked back to check on us advised the driver. Then, turning back to face the front, the driver started the van and headed to wherever we were going.

I signed as I changed positions and moved Matt so his head was in my lap. I sat there stroking his hair with one hand while my other hand rubbed down his arm. His skin was so hot to touch, and I worried that maybe he was reacting the tranquilliser. I didn't know enough about shifters or tranquillisers, for that matter, to be able to know how each would affect the other, but it did seem as though Matt's body was reacting in some way that didn't seem normal.

Matt stirred slightly but not loud enough for the thugs in the front to hear him. I leant down close to his ear and whispered, "Matt, if you can hear me, we are trapped in a van with three men being taken to God only knows where." I sighed and then continued, "I hope you're okay. You're burning up, and I don't know what to do."

Be strong, I told myself as emotions started to overwhelm me. The three thugs in the front started talking low to each other, but I caught parts of what they were saying.

It was my Uncle that had hired them, they were taking us to some safe house that was about an hour away, and they talked about how much of an arsehole my uncle was to deal with and how ruthless he had been to kill Dmitry so easily.

And John, I thought to myself as tears built in my eyes, John was my friend; he was a trained fighter. He could have defended himself, and he would have had he had time to. That meant that my uncle had snuck up on him. I had made John an easy target; he would have lowered his guard, believing it was just my Uncle and he was here to protect me, but that wasn't true at all. Tears ran down my cheeks thinking of how John would have suffered, and it was all my fault.

The bodies of the people I loved and cared about were adding up, and I wasn't sure how much more I could take; even innocent bystanders and colleagues were dead because of me and now Matt was unconscious, and we were being taken to god only knows where to have god only knows what done to us.

Just as I was beginning to descend into the rabbit hole of emotions, I felt Matt's hand reach up to grab the hand that was stroking his arm. When I looked down, Matt was staring up at me.

"What?" I whispered, shocked that Matt was awake. "How?" I asked, not wanting to draw the attention of the thugs in the front seat. Matt smiled up at me, and I leaned down towards him.

35

DETECTIVE MATTHEW ROCKLAN

A throbbing ache resonated through my skull, and I struggled to regain consciousness. My body shifted, and I became aware of a soft warmth beneath my head. As the fog in my mind cleared, I realized my head was cradled in Lily's lap. The gentle rise and fall of her breaths felt oddly comforting. Sweat trickled down my forehead, mingling with the persistent pain.

I groaned, stirring slightly. My arm felt heavy, but I lifted it and placed my hand on Lily's, which was tenderly stroking my arm. Her fingers were cold, betraying her anxiety.

Lily's eyes were wide with confusion, her lips forming a silent "what" as she stared down at me. Her voice barely a whisper, she leaned in closer, asking, "How?"

"Shh," I whispered back, not wanting to alert our captors. "I'm a wolf; my body burns off all drugs quickly." My words were slow and calm, thick with the grogginess that still clung to me.

Her gaze swept over me as she wiped it away using the back of her hand, the coolness of her skin soothing against my heated brow. The simple gesture brought a wave of gratitude and affection for this woman who still managed to show such tenderness despite the danger we were in.

"Hey," I said, my voice barely a whisper as I strained to gauge her reaction. "How long have we been driving?"

"About ten minutes," she replied quietly, her eyes darting around the dimly lit interior of the van. "I overheard them saying we're heading about an hour out of the city."

"An hour, huh?" My heart thundered in my chest, adrenaline beginning to course through my veins at the thought of what awaited us once we reached our destination. I knew I had to act quickly, but I needed to be sure I could handle the transformation first.

"Okay," I muttered, more to myself than to Lily. I closed my eyes and focused on the familiar sensation that accompanied my shift into wolf form. The raw power simmered just beneath the surface of my skin, tantalizingly close but not yet within my grasp. It was frustrating, like trying to catch a wisp of smoke with bare hands.

My fingers twitched involuntarily, their nails lengthening ever so slightly before retracting back to their human form. I clenched my fists, willing the change to come faster and give me the strength to protect us both. But it stubbornly refused to fully manifest, leaving me teetering on the edge of something powerful but ultimately unattainable.

As I met her gaze, I could see the fear swimming in her eyes, but there was determination there, too — a refusal to let this situation break her.

"Promise me you won't freak out," I murmured, my voice barely audible. "Once I shift, I will deal with these men and contact Sam via our pack link. But I promise, no matter what, I won't hurt you, okay?"

Lily hesitated momentarily; her lips pressed together in a thin line as she weighed the gravity of my words. Finally, she nodded, her grip on my hand tightening as if to anchor us together in whatever was about to unfold. "Okay," she whispered, the word barely more than a breath on the air between us.

I closed my eyes again, focusing all my energy on the change that still eluded me. The hum of the van's engine vibrated through my bones.

As I searched for the power within me, the wolf clawed at the edges of my consciousness. "Come on," I growled, teeth gritted in frustration. I rolled onto my stomach, not caring to draw attention to myself. The sensation of nails lengthening and fur sprouting across my body was familiar and strange, a stinging itch growing steadily more intense. My mouth stretched wide, fangs descending like the final curtain call of a grotesque performance.

"Matt..." Lily whispered, her voice trembling with uncertainty. She hesitated momentarily before reaching out and running her hand along my snout. I could feel the warmth of her touch even through the thick layer of fur, a reminder that she was trusting me.

I blew out a breath, summoning the pack link that connected me with Sam. "We're on the M5, I think. In a van. I'm about to crash it."

With that warning sent, I lunged forward, making a beeline for the driver's seat. The man barely had time to register my approach before my teeth sank into his throat, blood spurting hot and metallic between my jaws.

"Matt!" Lily cried out, but there was no turning back now. I whipped around to face the passenger, my movements swift and deadly. He reached for something – a weapon, perhaps – but I was too quick for him. My fangs found their mark, tearing through flesh and sinew with brutal efficiency.

The van veered off course, its tires screeching as it slid toward a concrete barrier. A heavy and suffocating sense of impending doom settled over me.

The world crashed around me, a cacophony of crumbling concrete and shattered glass. Then everything went black.

"MATT! MATT, COME ON, BUDDY!" SAM'S URGENT VOICE pulled me back from oblivion as pain seared through my body. I blinked opening my eyes, fighting the disorientation that threatened to drag me under again.

"Sam?" I croaked out, struggling to piece together what had happened. The van... Lily... I needed to find her. I tried to move, but the wreckage held me captive, an unwilling prisoner of twisted steel and jagged shards.

"Take it easy, Matt," Sam urged, gripping my arm as he began to pull me free of the wreckage. "We'll get you out of here."

"Where's Lily?" I demanded, gasping as my battered body protested even the slightest movement. But I couldn't afford to falter now. Not when she might still be in danger.

"Easy, man," Sam said, his voice tight with concern. "I don't know where she is. She wasn't here when we found you."

Panic clawed its way up my throat, threatening to choke me. My heart hammered against my ribcage, each beat echoing the frantic thought that raced through my mind: Where is she? Where is she?

"Are you sure?" I panted, adrenaline temporarily numbing the pain.

"What's happening," I pondered silently, lying motionless with a pounding head and heavy eyes. The rushing water filled my ears, prompting a groan as I shifted slightly, immediately regretting it. The air held a musty scent, and the persistent water flow continued unabated. Struggling to open my eyes, I squeezed them shut to muster strength, but they remained stubbornly shut. My body ached all over, fatigue weighing me down. Unable to articulate my current state, I tentatively reached out with my hands to explore my surroundings. The surface beneath me felt soft, like a mattress or sofa, until my hand brushed against cold metal. As I grasped the object and discerned its shape and texture, I realized it was a chain. Was I somehow chained to this mattress?

Panic threatened to overwhelm me, but I fought to maintain my composure. Racking my foggy mind for answers, I sternly demanded of myself, "Think Lily." Suddenly, a flash of Matt unconscious pierced through my thoughts, eliciting a gasp. Concern gripped me—was Matt injured? Another memory surged: Matt transformed into a majestic brown wolf before my eyes. His wolf form was as captivating as his human one. More memories flooded back—Matt bravely confronting our captors in his wolf form; the van accelerating dangerously as he grappled with the driver.

"Get to the back of the van," Matt's urgent command echoed in my mind as he reverted to human form. Following his instructions, I crawled towards the rear doors just as chaos erupted around us. Despite my intention to aid him, I froze at the sight through the front window—the van hurtling towards concrete barriers.

"Matt!" I screamed in terror.

"Stay back and hold on, Lily!" Matt's voice rang out amidst the turmoil as he battled our assailant up front. Then came the impact; everything blurred as Matt transformed once more into a wolf hurtling towards me before darkness consumed me.

"What happened to Matt?" Fear gripped me; tears streamed down my cheeks uncontrollably.

"Please be okay," I sobbed fervently, praying for his safety with every fibre of my being. Instinctively reaching for my mating mark, reassurance flooded over me—an overwhelming sense that Matt was alive coursed through me.

"I know you're safe," I whispered aloud in solace, willing myself to believe it wholeheartedly.

"Are you awake yet?" My uncle's voice shattered the silence from across the room.

"What do you want?" Emotionally masking my turmoil while addressing him.

"Oh! You're finally up," he retorted dismissively without acknowledging my query; his smirk practically palpable even without sight.

"What did you drug me with?" Frustration laced each word at my unresponsive limbs despite exerting effort.

He chuckled darkly. "Just a sedative; you'll be fine soon enough," his tone mocking as he drew closer.

"Stay away from me!" My bark carried all the force and defiance that physical restraint denied me.

He laughs again, "Don't worry, Lily. I have so many plans for you, and doing any of those things when you can't defend yourself is not my style," he states, venom reaching his tongue as he spits the words at me.

"No, you just get other people to do that sort of thing, right?" I spit back at him.

"Oh now, now," he tisks at me. "Dmitry really did have an obsession with you. I just encouraged it and gave him the little nudge he needed to take things to the next level." He lets out a loud laugh, and before I can ask him what's so funny, he continues.

"He actually thought that you would learn to love him," he tells me laughing again. "I tried to tell him not to get his hopes up, but he really was obsessed with making you his. So delusional in that way but he could crush your neck with one hand if he wanted to," he adds as he laughs again, finding the whole situation so amusing.

"You are crazy," I state.

"Oh, let's not be dramatic," he scoffs as I feel him sit on the mattress next to me.

I remain still, not wanting to alert him that I am scared even in the slightest. But I am; it's the scariest sensation not being able to open my eyes or barely move my body to defend myself or even see an attack coming. All my senses are on high alert and I can feel my heart rate has increased.

"Don't worry, Lily; this will all be over before you know it," he says, standing up and leaving the room.

I hear the door shut and blow out the breath I had been holding as a tear runs down my cheek. What was he planning to do to me? Was he really just going to kill me? I know the answer to that question, even if I don't want to believe it.

I paced Sam's office at the precinct, the worn-out carpet beneath my feet barely muffling my growls. My claws lengthened and retracted uncontrollably as fur sprouted along the back of my neck, only to retreat moments later. No matter how hard I tried, I couldn't stop the semi-change from happening.

"Matt," Sam said, his voice a mixture of concern and empathy. He watched me pace, his eyes locked onto mine every time I passed. He knew nothing would help; he'd been a lot like this after his wife had died. I knew it wasn't the same situation, but the sympathy in his eyes was familiar, similar to what I'd given him when his wife was gone and we could do nothing to help him heal.

"Damn it, Sam!" I snarled, slamming my fist on his desk. "We need to find her."

"I know, Matt," he replied softly. "We're doing everything we can."

"Everything?" I scoffed. "It's not enough!"

"Matt, please." Sam glanced around the room, making sure

no one else was watching. "You need to get a hold of yourself. You can't let them see you like this."

The steady tick-tock of the wall clock sounded like nails on a chalkboard as I stood there, my body feeling heavier with each passing second. I couldn't believe how quickly I was healing - or that I hadn't been hurt worse in the crash. The sickening crunch of metal and the jolt of pain as the car slammed into that cement partition played on a loop in my mind.

"Matt." Sam's voice broke through my thoughts. "how are you feeling?"

"Healing fast, all considering," I muttered, flexing my arms tentatively. My muscles still ached, but the sharp sting of broken bones had receded to a dull throb; I had always been a fast healer, but this time, I felt like I was healing quicker than normal. "Lucky me."

"Hey," Sam said softly, his eyes full of sympathy. "We'll find Lily. We have to keep our heads clear and stay focused."

"Focused, right." I tried to push away the image of Lily trapped in that van, her terrified eyes boring into mine as we were torn apart. Would she be okay? She'd been braced at the back of the van, but that wouldn't have stopped her from being thrown around like a rag doll.

When a sudden jolt of fear raced through me like a shockwave about an hour before, and I knew Lily had woken up. The sensation was so intense that my claws started to lengthen and retract involuntarily, fur sprouting along the back of my neck before retreating just as quickly. It was impossible to stop this semi-shift from happening; her terror called out to the wolf in me, urging me to protect her. Her heart raced, then slowed, then raced again, causing mine to follow suit.

"Found anything else?." Sam turned to Henry, who had

been hunched over his laptop, reviewing the highway footage from the safety camera. "Any leads?"

"Right after the crash, an SUV pulled up next to the van," Henry explained, his voice shaking slightly. "They ripped the back door open and... and pulled Lily out. She was unconscious when they bundled her into the back of their car and took off."

"Damn it," I cursed under my breath, clenching my fists at my sides. "We need to find them."

"Agreed," said Sam, his voice tight with determination. "Any idea where they might've gone?"

"Unfortunately not," Henry admitted, his frustration evident. "The SUV didn't have a number plate, and the windows were blacked out. The kidnappers wore all black too, making it difficult to identify them."

"Keep digging, Henry," Sam urged. "Every little bit helps."

"Of course," Henry nodded, turning back to his computer, his fingers flying across the keyboard as he continued searching for anything that could lead us to Lily.

"Matt, we'll find her," Sam reassured me, touching my shoulder. "We won't stop until we do."

"Thanks, Sam," I said, swallowing hard against the lump in my throat. "I just... can't lose her."

"I know," he replied softly. "Just remember what I told you before: You're not just a wolf. You're a detective, a friend, and one hell of a partner. And Lily needs you now more than ever. Stay strong for her."

"Always."

Turning to Henry as he typed away, I asked, "Any luck tracing the SUV?"

"Nothing yet," Henry sighed.

"Damn it," I growled under my breath, clenching my fists. Thoughts raced through my mind as I tried to figure out where they could have taken her. It was maddening, feeling so helpless and powerless.

My gaze fixed on Henry as he scoured the safety camera footage, a desperate hope igniting in my chest. His sandy blonde hair was dishevelled from running his hands through it countless times, and his blue eyes revealed frustration.

"Campbelltown exit," Henry said suddenly, breaking the tense silence over us. "The SUV took the Campbelltown exit, but beyond that, I can't find anything."

"Damn it," I muttered, my fists clenching involuntarily. The thought that they could have switched cars and vanished like smoke only heightened the urgency gnawing at me. "What now?"

"Keep looking," Sam replied, his voice firm yet weary. "We'll go through every frame of footage we can find. Someone has to have seen something."

"Right," I agreed, taking a deep breath to steady myself. I knew I wasn't strong enough yet to follow the link between Lily and me - not with the injuries I had sustained. All I needed was time to heal and for Lily to feel a surge of fear so I could pinpoint her location. The mere thought sickened me, but it was our best shot at finding her.

I leaned against a wall, desperation clawing at my insides as I fought to keep control over my shifting form. Clenching my fists, I tried to focus on anything other than the fear that threatened to consume me.

"Matt," Sam's voice cut through the haze, pulling me back

to the present. "We're doing everything we can, you know that."

"I know," I replied, forcing the words out through gritted teeth. "But it's not enough. We need to find her, Sam. Before it's too late."

"Hey, man, don't talk like that," Henry chimed in, his blue eyes filled with concern. "We won't let anything happen to Lily."

"Easy for you to say," I muttered, my heart pounding in my chest. "You don't know what it's like - feeling her fear, knowing she's out there somewhere, terrified and alone." As much as I appreciated their support, I couldn't shake the feeling that time was running out.

"Matt, look at me," Sam said softly, his eyes locking onto mine. "I know it's hard, but you have to stay strong. For Lily."

"Strong?" I scoffed, the sound bitter. "What good is being strong when I can't even protect her?"

"Strength isn't just about muscle, Matt," Sam continued, his voice steady. "It's about perseverance. It's about refusing to give up, no matter how hopeless things may seem."

"Sam's right," Henry added, nodding solemnly. "We'll find her, Matt. And when we do, her uncle will pay for what he's done."

Their words echoed in my head, a glimmer of hope amidst the darkness. I knew they were right - I had to keep going, for Lily's sake. If I lost her, I wouldn't be able to go on. I couldn't live like Sam, carrying the weight of loss with me every day.

As we resumed our search, I found myself clinging to that small sliver of hope, feeding off its strength as I fought against the panic that threatened to overwhelm me. I knew that finding Lily was the only thing that mattered now - for both of us.

Her uncle would pay for what he'd done, and I would ensure it. Because without her, life wasn't worth living. And I refused to let that be our fate.

38

LILY JAMES

I lay there for what felt like days but had likely only been a few hours. I was starting to get some feeling back in my feet and legs, which was a relief. I was also now able to open my eyes, well, open them as far as they would open. My left eye was swollen and sore, and I knew I must have looked like I had gone 12 rounds and didn't take the win but was knocked out cold. I had been able to check out my surroundings now. I was in what looked to be an old wine cellar; there was racking for wine, but it was all empty. The floor was made of dark slate tiles that were cool to the touch. I was indeed on a mattress in the corner of the room and chained by my ankle to the racking. I had tried yanking on the chain, but I didn't have the strength yet to tell how secure it was.

I was still so damn tired, and I was now struggling to keep my eyes open. I couldn't tell if it was day or night, which made me so uneasy. I had no way of tracking time to know how long I had been here. Just as my thoughts were starting to get away from me, the door to the cellar opened. It wasn't my uncle but another man dressed all in black. He had a hat on, and I couldn't really see what he looked like as the lighting down here was dimmed and scarce. I could tell he was looking over in my direction, but I don't think he could tell if I was awake or not from where he was standing.

"Are you awake?" he asked, confirming my suspicions.

"What's it to you?" I snapped at him without even moving.

He chuckled, "Just checking in," he stated as he turned and walked back out of the cellar.

I sighed; I figured he was only checking to make sure I was still alive.

It had been a few hours since my uncle's last visit, so I figured it would be another few until someone came to check on me again. Thinking it was an opportune time, I decided to close my eyes and get some rest. Exhausted and emotionally and physically drained, I let myself drift off to sleep.

A loud bang jolted me awake sometime later. Instinctively, I tried to sit up to see what had happened but found that I still didn't have full movement in my body nor enough strength to sit up on my own.

"Sorry, did we wake you?" My uncle's voice echoed from the other side of the room. Remaining silent, alertness washed over me as I pondered his intentions. A chill ran down my spine as I attempted to stay calm. Truth be told, fear gripped me tightly but there was no way he'd know that.

"What? Not talking to your favourite Uncle?" He cooed with a smirk spreading across his face as he moved closer towards me.

I stared at him right in the eyes, attempting to convey the depth of hate and disgust I now harbored for him. He returned my gaze with a look of resentment and anger.

"You really do look like your mother," he stated after a few moments of our silent confrontation. "She was very beautiful just like you," he added as his hand reached down to touch my cheek.

"Don't touch me," I spit at him, pulling away as if his touch has burnt me. In a way, it has; I despise this man and can't stand him touching me or being anywhere near me. He's betrayed his entire family out of jealousy.

"You're feisty, just like her," he laughs, moving away from my side towards the back wall. I glance over my shoulder, trying to discern his intentions but he's turned his back on me, obscuring everything.

"I wonder," he muses with his back still turned to me, "how much pain someone so feisty could withstand?" As he turns around to face me again, I see a whip in his right hand. My eyes follow its movement as he strides towards me, caressing the strands with his left hand.

"This beauty right here loves to inflict pain without causing too much damage," he chuckles darkly. "Well, not enough to kill you anyway – just enough to make you wish you were dead."

He stared at me again, as if assessing my reaction or waiting for me to crack and show him any sign that I was scared. But I refused to give him anything. I ordered my heart rate to slow so I could keep my breathing at a normal rate, and I stared back at him, not even blinking. He was not going to break me. I was going to be strong for myself, for my parents, for John and for Matt.

"Roll her over and rip open her top at the back; remove the chain so I can watch her squirm," he ordered the other men in the room.

I didn't fight them as they did what they had been told to

do; I needed to save my strength. The air felt cold against my skin when my shirt was ripped open, and goosebumps formed on my arms and back.

I could hear him walk over beside me once the other men were done. He was hitting the whip up against his thigh; he was trying to intimidate me, trying to scare me, trying to get any reaction out of me. But I remained as calm as I could on the outside while my insides churned in fear of what was yet to come.

I knew it was going to hurt—that much was a given—but it was not knowing how much or for how long this torture would continue that bothered me most.

"Don't worry, I'll start off slowly," he said darkly his evil side clearly coming out now that even he couldn't hide it in his tone.

I simply closed my eyes and buried my face against the mattress waiting for the first whip. Seconds later I heard him take in a sharp breath and I felt the whoosh of air as the whip came down and struck me right across my back. I gasped as the realisation of just how painful it was, my back felt like it was burning and the pain just wouldn't go away. I held my breath hoping that would somehow ease the pain but it didn't.

Then a second whip hit across my back and I cried out slightly not expecting the second one so soon after the first but I didn't have long to even process, as a third strike occurred and then a fourth and fifth.

Now I knew I had cried out loud, unable to control my reaction to the pain that was coming so swiftly and frequently. Tears streamed down my cheeks while my breathing grew heavy and rapid. I tried to catch my breath, but the pain was simply too overwhelming. I could hear his breathing as well, also ragged and heavy. But with each strike against my back, I could hear his chuckles of enjoyment at my pain. He was deriving pleasure from this, and that was the only thing preventing me from begging him to stop. I wouldn't give him the satisfaction of hearing me beg; I would rather die than give him that pleasure.

I lost count of the hits after a while, teetering on the brink of unconsciousness from the pain. Every inch of me throbbed and I no longer had the strength to bury my face in my hands. Instead, I just lay there, with my head turned to one side and tears streaming down my cheeks. Blood was trickling down the side of my body from my back – a chilling reminder of how many times I'd been whipped. But then, almost mercifully, he stopped. He dropped the whip and left without uttering a single word. Left me lying there, relieved that it was over but also strangely grateful that he hadn't broken me enough to make me beg for mercy. With a final blink, I let the darkness and exhaustion take over as everything faded into blackness.

39

DETECTIVE MATTHEW ROCKLAN

Sam had sent me home about three hours ago, practically shoving me out the door. "Matt, you need to rest," he insisted, his face etched with concern. "You're walking a hole into my office floor."

"Fine," I muttered, knowing he was right. The last thing I needed was to lose control at work. So, I had taken up walking one through the carpet of my apartment instead.

As I paced back and forth like a caged animal, the worn carpet beneath my feet did little to quiet the storm in my head. If anything, it only reminded me of how desperate I was to find Lily and bring her home safely. I clenched my fists, feeling the frustration build inside me.

"Damn it!" I growled, slamming my fist against the wall. I couldn't shake the feeling that time was running out and we were no closer to finding her than when she first disappeared.

The scent of Lily still hung in the air like a haunting melody, tendrils of her perfume wrapping themselves around me as I walked around our apartment. My heart constricted at the sight of the police tape stretched across the door, a cruel reminder that she was gone – stolen from our sanctuary.

"Matt, don't let this get to you," Liam's voice echoed in my head from earlier, but it was easier said than done. With every step around, the absence of Lily grew heavier, a crushing weight on my chest.

I paced back and forth, trying to find some semblance of control in a situation that had spiralled out of my grasp.

My heart raced as I pondered our next move. We were facing a daunting challenge in rescuing her, and my mind was scattered with different possibilities. Despite my injuries having fully healed, I still couldn't establish a connection through our link to locate her. Our team had been aided by the entire police department, but we had to adhere to protocol and couldn't risk exposing our true identities to other officers. We had meticulously crafted a plan for navigating the maze of bureaucratic red tape in order to find Lily, but even with all our preparations, she remained elusive. It was like trying to catch a fleeting dream or grasp smoke between your fingers.

My heart ached for Lily, but my mind was in pieces, trying to focus on what needed to be done. The police tape across the front door had broken my heart when I walked through it earlier. It felt like a cold reminder of our current reality.

"Stay calm," I whispered to myself, but my words held little comfort. My wolf paced restlessly inside me, anxious and tense. We both needed something to hold onto, some semblance of peace amidst the chaos.

I found myself standing in the doorway of our bedroom, the sight of Lily's belongings strewn everywhere making the pain in my chest intensify. Moving boxes cluttered the room, their contents half-unpacked as if frozen in time. I stepped inside, my eyes drawn to a pile of her clothes spilling out from one of the boxes.

"Damn it, Lily," I muttered, my voice trembling. I scooped up a handful of her shirts and held them close to my face, breathing in deeply. The scent of her filled my nostrils, and for a moment, I could almost feel her presence. It calmed my wolf just enough, allowing me to think more clearly.

"Okay, focus," I told myself, forcing the pain and worry to the back of my mind. "We'll find her. We have to."

Just then, an agonizing, sharp pain lashed across my back, so intense that it brought me to my knees. It felt like my entire back was engulfed in flames, the searing heat threatening to consume me. And then, without warning, it came again and again, each wave more unbearable than the last.

"Shit!" I gasped, struggling to breathe through the pain. My body convulsed, and I couldn't stop the transformation. My clothes ripped apart as my bones shifted and fur erupted from my skin. I collapsed onto the floor, now fully in wolf form, panting heavily.

"Damn it, not now!" I growled to myself, trying to regain control. But even as my thoughts raced, the pain continued to lash at me like a whip, a relentless assault that threatened to break me.

Suddenly, amidst the pain, a vision flickered in my mind — an image of a dark, abandoned cellar surrounded by overgrown weeds and tall, rusted fences. The location was familiar; it was still in the Campbelltown area. A faint scent of her drifted through the air, mingling with the smell of dampness and decay.

"Alpha," I called out through our pack mind link, struggling to keep my thoughts coherent as the pain continued to tear at me. "I know where she is. Campbelltown. At the Old Millhouse, on Queens St."

"Matt, you need to transform back," Sam's steady and commanding voice said. Get dressed. We'll put together a tactical team. Henry's on his way to pick you up."

"Right," I agreed, gritting my teeth against the pain. I focused all my energy on pushing my wolf back down, forcing it to retreat into the depths of my being. It was a battle of wills that I couldn't afford to lose.

I stood there, trembling, as sweat dripped from every pore. My body ached, and my mind screamed in protest, but I had to shift back. The wolf inside me snarled, resisting the change, but I couldn't let it win—not now.

"Damn you," I hissed through gritted teeth, forcing my human form to resurface inch by painfully inch. The beast within fought back savagely, unwilling to relinquish control, but I wouldn't be denied. Lily needed me—now more than ever.

Bones cracked and reformed, muscles twisted and contorted, and finally, I was human again. Exhausted and shaking, I threw on some fresh clothes, not caring whether they matched. The holster belt followed, along with a bulletproof vest—just in case things went south.

"Come on, Henry," I muttered, glancing at the door, my impatience growing with each passing second. I couldn't afford to waste any more time. Every moment I stood here was another moment Lily was in danger.

As if on cue, tires screeched outside, and I raced out the front door, taking the stairs two at a time. My heart pounded in my chest as I reached the street, leaping into Henry's beat-up Honda without waiting for it to come to a stop.

"Go!" I barked, gripping the door handle so tightly my knuckles turned white.

"Chill, dude. We'll get her back," Henry said, giving me a reassuring grin as he floored the gas pedal. The car roared to life, speeding off towards Campbelltown.

My phone rang then, and I answered it without thinking. Two minutes of dead air followed, but I knew what it meant—an untraceable call, part of the plan. God, this was all so convoluted.

"Thanks, Henry," I said quietly, hanging up the phone and staring out the window. The streets blurred together, a somber backdrop to my racing thoughts.

"Anytime, man," he replied, his sandy blonde hair catching the fleeting glow of streetlights as we sped past.

Hold on, Lily. I'm coming for you, my love. And heaven help anyone who tries to stop me.

40

LILY JAMES

Life can be so cruel sometimes. Those words echoed through my mind as I slept. I dreamt of a future that could have been one where my parents were alive. In this dream, I met Matt and introduced him to my amazing, kind, and caring parents. They loved him and blessed us to marry when Matt asked for it. My dad clasped Matt on the shoulder, joking about being unable to give me back once he realized what a handful I was. My mum slapped my dad's arm playfully as she sat beside him while Matt laughed and shot me a wink from across the room. It was such a beautiful moment that tears streamed down my face, even in sleep. But that moment would never happen; my parents were dead. I was pretty sure that my uncle planned to kill me at his earliest convenience, lead Matt and the others to my lifeless body, and then disappear into the night without leaving any trace behind.

Matt would spend the rest of his life trying to hunt down my uncle. He would waste his life seeking revenge for me. Perhaps one day, he would find my uncle and kill him. I knew this, but my Uncle's death wouldn't cure the anger and pain of losing his mate. Matt would end up broken, without focus, once his quest for revenge was complete. I didn't want to think about Matt being unable to move on with his life without me, yet images of him sad and alone kept playing in my mind.

I couldn't afford to think like this and willed my body to wake up. Slowly but surely, I began to regain consciousness, though my body ached and my back felt as if it were on fire. I attempted to move.

"Aah!" I cried out as intense pain ripped through my entire body.

I lay still on the floor, scanning the room. A light had been left on in the back corner, illuminating the room more than it had been since I arrived. Underneath this light was a tray; although I couldn't see what was on it from where I lay, I knew that whatever it held could be used for protection.

I looked around for the chain attached to my leg and noted that it was still off; they had forgotten to put it back on. I sucked in a breath and pulled myself along the mattress as carefully as possible, trying not to let the pain overwhelm me so I wouldn't pass out again and attempting not to make too much noise to alert anyone that I was moving around. The pain was so intense it felt like I was being whipped all over again, but I gritted my teeth and cursed under my breath each time pain shot through me. Slowly, I crawled off the stained mattress; the angle I had to position my body for this movement almost overwhelmed me.

I continued to drag myself along the ground, determined to reach the tray, even if it was my last act. Once I reached the tray, I paused beneath it to catch my breath and brace myself for the impending pain of reaching up. I closed my eyes and took five deep breaths, attempting to push the pain to the back of my mind. Then, without hesitation, I opened my eyes, reached up for the tray and placed my hand on it. Carefully but swiftly, I began feeling around its contents.

My hand brushed against something metallic, and I nicked my finger. The sharp sting of the cut registered immediately, but I didn't retract my hand. Instead, I moved it further down the object, tracing its form with my fingertips to confirm what I thought it was. "Scalpel," I muttered to myself, sighing in relief. A scalpel was useful; it was a tool with which I could defend myself and inflict damage if necessary. My fingers closed around its base, gripping it tightly as I withdrew my hand from the tray, bringing the scalpel along with me.

Now came the excruciating task of crawling back to the mattress without arousing suspicion. As I gritted my teeth and started moving, I couldn't decide if having the scalpel made me feel better about my predicament. But one thing was certain - the pain seemed less intense on this return journey. Either that or each movement was causing further nerve damage, resulting in a loss of feeling and sensation in certain areas.

Within a few minutes, I had returned to the mattress. Painfully and slowly, I hauled myself back onto it and then laid down. My aim was not only to find the most comfortable position but also to make me appear asleep while allowing me to act at any potential threat. Despite my exhaustion and intense pain, I refused to let my guard down; I wouldn't be caught off guard again like before. So, I forced myself to stay awake.

I didn't have to wait long until I heard someone descending the stairs. Preparing myself for what was about to come, I concealed the scalpel in my right hand. It would cause discomfort when turning on my back from this position, but it offered the best combination of force and concealment under these circumstances.

With my eyes shut, I lay in wait as the footsteps hurried down the stairs - faster than before. They halted momentarily at the foot of the stairs before proceeding again after a brief pause.

Now, they were strolling towards me. Were they shocked by the damage they'd inflicted, or did they think I was already dead and dreaded having to break the news to my uncle, who wasn't finished with me yet? Regardless, I waited. I bided my time until they were above me, then launched my attack.

Quick as a flash, I rolled over and lunged at the person who had come to check on me with the scalpel. A scream tore from my throat as pain seared through my back, but I poured all of my strength into stabbing them. They were too quick, though, stepping back just in time.

I only managed to nick their arm; my vision blurred from the pain caused me to completely misjudge the distance. Undeterred, I tried again to thrust the scalpel in their direction.

"Back off," I roared with as much force as possible. "I'll stab you!"

"Lily, it's me," Matt's voice resonates.

"Matt?" I question, rubbing my eyes in an attempt to see him.

"It's me, baby," he assures me. His blurry figure approaches, and I can discern his shape. "I'm going to take the scalpel from you, okay?"

My fingers tighten around the scalpel. Despite his words, I'm not entirely convinced it's him, and I want to be prepared for anything. However, when his fingers contact my hand, a wave of recognition washes over me - it is him. An immediate sense of calm pervades my body, and I loosen my grip on the scalpel, allowing Matt to take it from me.

He carefully places the scalpel on the ground. As I rub my eyes to see him more clearly, he moves closer still. Kneeling before him now, he cradles my face in his hands and presses his forehead against mine - a gesture that triggers an emotional breakdown within me.

"You found me," I sob out loud as he gently holds onto my shoulders and inches closer still. He consciously tries not to touch my back but strives to comfort me as best he can.

"I would never have stopped until I found you, Lily," Matt whispers into my ear softly - a promise that rings true in every syllable of his words.

"Never," he reaffirms; this time, there's no doubt left in me - he is telling the truth.

41

The metallic scent filled my nostrils as I scooped Lily up into my arms, her bloodied back pressed against my chest. I didn't have to ask what happened; I could make a pretty good guess from how she trembled in my grasp.

"Listen, Lily," I said, trying to keep my voice steady despite the fear gnawing at me. "We're not safe yet. Backup hasn't arrived, and I broke protocol coming in here to find you."

Her eyes widened, and I could see the flicker of panic behind them. She clung to me, her small hands gripping my shirt like a lifeline. I couldn't blame her – I was just as scared. But I needed to be strong for the both of us right now.

"Matt, what if they find us before your team arrives?" Her voice quivered, barely above a whisper.

"Then we'll handle it," I replied, trying to sound more confident than I felt. "But right now, we need to focus on getting out of here."

With Lily securely in my arms, I moved through the crumbling basement, each step a calculated risk. The place was old, its foundation weakened over time, and I couldn't trust it to hold up much longer. If I hadn't been so desperate to save Lily, I wouldn't have come anywhere near this death trap.

The creaking groan of the wooden stairs echoed ominously through the building as I cautiously climbed, one careful step at a time. The ancient structure felt like it could collapse at any moment, and I couldn't help but wince at the thought of being buried under the rubble with Lily in my arms.

"Matt," she murmured, her voice barely audible. "Will we make it out?"

"Of course we will," I reassured her, though my doubts gnawed at me. "Just hang on tight."

Lily's fragile body was pressed tightly against my chest, legs carefully tucked up to avoid scraping against the grimy walls. Her blood-stained back was a constant reminder of the horrors she'd endured, and it only fuelled my determination to get her to safety.

As my footsteps echoed through the dimly lit stairwell, Lily's voice trembled with fear. "Matt, where's my uncle?"

"Can't be sure," I admitted, my heart pounding. "Henry caused a distraction so I could slip in and find you. But don't worry, we'll figure it out."

A sudden burst of gunfire ripped through the air, followed by the thundering footsteps of someone charging towards us. My pulse quickened, adrenaline surging as I clutched Lily tighter.

"Shit," I muttered, racing up the remaining steps with newfound urgency. The old building groaned around us, its age evident in the creaking floorboards and peeling wallpaper.

We burst into an old-fashioned kitchen, stone floors slick with dampness and rows of metal benches rusted from years of neglect. The remnants of a once-thriving restaurant lay abandoned, awaiting demolition.

As I set Lily down on her feet, the musty, abandoned kitchen felt thick with tension. The rancid smell of mold and decaying food lingered in my nostrils, but all I could focus on was keeping us alive.

"Get down," I whispered sharply, pulling my gun from its holster with a quick motion. I could feel the cold metal press into my palm as my fingers wrapped around the grip. "Stay low and stay quiet."

"Okay," she replied, her voice barely audible. Her wide eyes met mine momentarily before she crouched down behind one of the old, rusty metal benches. The fear in her gaze tore at my heart, but I had no time to offer comfort.

The sound of heavy footsteps grew louder, echoing off the dilapidated walls. My heartbeat pounded in my ears, drowning out everything else. As a man I didn't recognize burst through the door, his face contorted in rage, I steadied my aim and squeezed the trigger.

"Shit," I muttered under my breath, my chest heaving as I watched the man's lifeless body crumple to the ground, a bullet hole in his forehead. The loud blast of the gunshot still rang in my ears, but there was no time to dwell on it. We had to keep moving.

"Come on," I said urgently, reaching out to Lily. She grasped it tightly, her small, trembling fingers intertwining with mine. "We have to go. Now."

We raced towards the back door together, our footsteps echoing off the grimy stone floor. The taste of fear and desperation filled the stale air around us, bitter and sharp like the coppery tang of blood.

"Matt, are we going to make it out of here?" Lily asked, panic lacing her words. As much as I wanted to reassure her, to promise her safety, I couldn't find the words. All I knew was I would do everything I could to protect her.

"Stay close to me," I told her instead, my voice strained with emotion. "We're a team. We'll figure this out together."

The door loomed before us, an ominous barrier to freedom. Chained shut and weathered from years of neglect, it looked like it hadn't been opened in decades.

"Shit," I muttered under my breath, the weight of our situation pressing down on my chest like a ton of bricks. Lily glanced up at me, her eyes wide with fear, and I could see the silent plea in them. We couldn't give up now, not when we'd come so far.

"Stay back," I told her, positioning myself in front of the door. With every ounce of strength, I repeatedly threw my shoulder into the heavy wood. The frame began to splinter and crack like gunfire in the tense silence. "Come on, you piece of shit," I growled through gritted teeth, sweat beading on my forehead as I continued my assault on the stubborn door.

Finally, with a triumphant roar, the door gave way, sending me stumbling out into the cool air. The breeze greeted me like a balm on my overheated skin, but there was no time to savor it. I turned back towards Lily, extending my hand to help her out of the crumbling building.

"Let's go!" I shouted, grabbing her hand tightly as she raced out behind me. Together, we sprinted away from the decrepit structure, our breathing ragged and laboured as adrenaline coursed through our veins.

The cold air whipped across my face as we sprinted, our

feet pounding against the worn cobblestone. The once lively outdoor dining area now stood abandoned and lonely.

"Matt, I don't know if I can keep running," Lily panted, her voice strained with exhaustion.

"Stay close to me, Lily," I whispered, trying to keep my fear at bay. "We're almost out of here."

Our path to freedom was suddenly cut off as we rounded the corner. Lily's uncle and several armed men emerged from the shadows, their guns raised and ready. A chill ran down my spine, and I knew that there was no way we could outrun them.

"Nice try," her uncle sneered, his eyes filled with malice. "But it's simply not happening."

"Please, let her go," I begged, my voice cracking under my desperation. "She doesn't deserve this."

"Tomato, tomato," he replied coldly, his finger tightening on the trigger.

As Lily's uncle smirked, I caught sight of a large wolf slinking behind him. My heart leaped with hope - it was Henry. Our eyes locked, and I knew he was ready to act.

"Matt?" Lily whispered, sensing my change in demeanor.

"Trust me," I murmured, holding three fingers at my side, our secret signal for shifting. The tactical team had to be nearby; we couldn't afford to be seen in our wolf forms.

"Wh-what are you doing?" she stammered, her voice wobbling with fear.

"Getting us out of here," I replied, gripping the gun tightly as I passed it to her. "No matter what happens, don't stop running."

"Okay," she breathed, nodding hesitantly as she took the weapon.

My other hand now displayed two fingers, and I felt my

body beginning to tingle, the sensations of shifting coursing through me. I focused, preparing myself for what was about to come.

"Last chance, boy," her uncle warned, his voice icy and devoid of compassion.

"Go to hell," I spat, my fingers dropping to one, and I could feel my body morphing, bones snapping and muscles contorting as I transformed into my wolf form. The last thing I saw before my vision changed was Lily's wide, terrified eyes.

I lunged for her uncle, my powerful legs propelling me forward with incredible speed. In my peripheral vision, I saw Henry pounce on one of the hired men. Then, I heard it – the sharp 'pop-pop' of a gun, followed by a man's body crumpling to the ground. Lily had kept her promise.

The taste of blood filled my mouth as my fangs sank into her uncle's neck, and I bit down with all my might. The metallic tang was overwhelming, but I refused to let go until I knew he was no longer a threat.

"Run, Lily," I thought, praying she'd understand our fight wasn't over yet. As her footsteps faded into the distance, I turned my attention to the remaining enemies – and the inevitable chaos ahead.

42

The pain was intense, my back throbbing with each beat of my heart, but I refused to let it hinder our escape. As we rounded the corner and came face-to-face with my uncle and his horde of armed men, a wave of despair washed over me. I felt an overwhelming urge to both cry and gouge out my uncle's eyes simultaneously. We had been on the brink of freedom, so close to slipping away, but yet again, my uncle had managed to stay one step ahead. Matt exchanged words with him, and I knew it was only a matter of time before gunshots would fill the air once more. Closing my eyes for just a moment, I tried to suppress the pain and torment consuming me at that moment. Then I sensed it - somehow, inexplicably - the moment Matt realised that the tables had turned in our favour.

"Matt," I whispered, trying to discern what had shifted. Yet, nothing seemed different to me; we were still in deep trouble. "Trust me," Matt insisted. Of course, I did trust him, but I didn't want him risking his life. If that was his plan, then count me out. I needed more details; and assurance he wasn't about to do something reckless because living without him wasn't an option for me. "Getting us out of here," Matt replied as he handed the gun over to me. That's when it hit me - the change. Matt was altering our formation. "No matter what happens, don't stop running." He fixed his gaze on mine, and it was as if I could see his strategy through his eyes. It felt like the best shot we had under the circumstances.

I was determined to have Matt's back and protect him for as long as possible. With a quick nod of reassurance, the plan sprung into action. Everything unfolded rapidly; when Matt transformed into his wolf form and attacked, a second wolf joined in. I noticed my uncle's men reacting late to the situation, allowing me to strike.

I targeted the fastest among them, aiming my gun at him just as he aimed his at Matt. I pulled the trigger, watching as the bullet hit him square in the chest. This gave Matt and the other wolf enough time to counterattack. I observed as Matt sunk his teeth into my uncle's neck - he wouldn't release until he was certain my uncle had no chance of survival.

That's when I took off running. My adrenaline surged, pushing aside any pain or fear. I sprinted towards the car, screaming for Sam at the gate. His vehicle screeched to a halt, and he was out of it faster than lightning could strike. I practically collapsed into his arms from exhaustion.

"Matt! And the other!" I shouted at Sam while pointing in their direction.

"Stay here," Sam instructed, swiftly seating me in his car before calling Miles to follow him. "Please be okay," I muttered aloud, not necessarily to anyone or anything specific. I needed to voice it, hoping the universe would heed my plea. I yearned for a different outcome this time, unlike the last when I had lost everything - my parents, my family, my entire damn way of life. This time needed to be different; I needed the demise of the man who had ruined my existence.

I yearned for the safety of the man I loved and finally being able to move on from the darkest period of my life without constantly glancing over my shoulder every waking moment. As I sat there in the car, with adrenaline subsiding and pain resurfacing in my back, my thoughts began to wander off into a reel of memories from the past twelve months or so.

They played out like a movie in my mind: flashes of all that I had endured repeated themselves endlessly – an abundance of darkness, sorrow and pain. But then images of Matt began to replace these grim scenes with light; loneliness was replaced by feelings of belonging to a family, and pain was substituted by the love that Matt had given me even in such a short span. A tear trickled down my cheek as warmth washed over me just as pain seized control again and caused me to black out.

43

DETECTIVE MATTHEW ROCKLAN

I could still taste the iron tang of blood in my mouth as I stood there, naked and exposed. Killing half a dozen men in wolf form was easy; explaining why I was stark naked when the tactical team found me wouldn't be.

"Matt, we need to move," Henry whispered urgently, his sandy blonde hair ruffled from our recent... activities. He was right. The second the men and Lily's uncle were dead, Henry and I grabbed our ripped clothes with our teeth and raced back to his beat-up Honda. Spare clothes - we always had them stashed in the trunk for this situation.

"Damn, it's freezing," I grumbled, clutching the tattered remains of my jeans in one hand.

"Quit complaining and get dressed," Henry snapped, tossing me a spare set of clothes.

"Thanks," I mumbled, pulling on the ill-fitting shorts and T-shirt. The clothes were tight, but they'd have to do.

"Anytime," Henry replied, already dressed and scanning the area for any signs of the tactical team. "We need to hurry."

"Right." With one last glance at the carnage we'd left behind, I slammed the trunk closed, and we took off again.

Henry and I sprinted back to the scene, my heart pounding. The borrowed clothes clung uncomfortably to my skin.

"Damn," I muttered under my breath, the too-tight fabric making it difficult to take full strides.

"Focus, Matt," Henry shot back, his voice tense and low.

As we rounded the corner, Sam appeared, eyes wide with disbelief. "Lily's in my car," he panted, pointing towards his vehicle. "She's safe."

"Thank God," I whispered, relief flooding through me.

Sam's gaze shifted to the lifeless men scattered across the ground. "Shit," he muttered, furrowing his brow. "Wolves do not frequent this area at all."

I interjected, my mind racing. "How are we going to explain all this?" I could see the concern etched on Sam's face and knew we had to act fast.

"Sam," I called out, trying to steady my voice. "How far out is the tactical team?"

"Five minutes, max," he replied, glancing at his watch.

"Gas explosion?" I offered, hoping the suggestion would be enough to cover our tracks.

"Good idea," he nodded, understanding what must be done. "Let's make it quick."

As we moved into action, grabbing the bodies of the men we'd killed in wolf form, a sick feeling gnawed at my insides. This wasn't how things were supposed to go—Lily shouldn't have been caught up in this.

"Help me with this one," Henry grunted as he struggled to drag one of the larger men towards the building. I hurried over, feeling the weight of the man's dead body in my hands as we hauled him inside.

"Are we going to get away with this?" I thought, a knot of anxiety tightening in my chest. My hands trembled as I wiped the sweat from my brow.

"Alright," Sam barked, directing us as we positioned the bodies inside and outside the kitchen. This should do it."

"Let's hope so," I muttered, the enormity of our actions settling in like a lead weight.

As we retreated, I couldn't help but wonder if we'd ever truly escape the consequences of this. The lingering taste of blood in my mouth served as a bitter reminder of who—and what—I was.

The gas burners hissed as Henry turned them on, the gas slowly filling the room.

"Cover your ears," he warned, shouldering his weapon. With a sharp crack, he fired a single round into the gas cylinder outside. Contrary to popular belief, gas cylinders don't explode when shot at; they simply leak gas, which needs a spark to ignite. As the smell of gas filled the air outside, I felt my pulse race with anticipation and anxiety.

"Make it quick, Miles," Sam urged, his voice tense. Miles rummaged in his pocket for a cigarette lighter, his hands shaking slightly. He tore a strip of cloth from one of the dead men's shirts, lit it on fire, and tossed it toward the leaking gas.

"Run!" he shouted, and we all bolted away from the building. My heart hammered in my chest as we sprinted, my breath coming in short gasps. Halfway back to Sam's car, I heard the tactical team's vehicles approaching at breakneck speed.

"Damn it," I muttered, glancing over my shoulder just as the old building exploded behind us. The force of the blast flung us forward, our bodies slamming hard onto the unforgiving asphalt. The world spun around me; everything was reduced to a blur of pain and panic.

"Is everyone okay?" Sam's voice cut through the ringing in my ears, but I could barely form a coherent thought, let alone respond. All I could think about was Lily—where was she? Was she safe?

"Matt, answer me!" Sam's hand gripped my arm, jolting me back to reality. I forced a weak nod, trying to ignore the throbbing pain in every inch of my body.

"Fine...I'm fine," I managed to croak, the words tasting like ash in my mouth.

"Where's...Lily?" I forced the words past gritted teeth, my heart heavy with worry. The bond we shared reassured me she was alive, but the uncertainty gnawed at me relentlessly.

"Safe," Sam replied, his eyes darting between me and the inferno raging behind us. "She's still in my car."

"Good," I muttered, relief washing over me like a cold shower—sharp, biting, yet comforting.

As the tactical team reached us, one pulled out a radio and urgently called for the fire brigade. I lay there on the unforgiving ground, letting them tend to us while praying that the flames would consume any evidence of our monstrous transformations. That the stray bullet Miles had fired into the gas cylinder could be written off as friendly fire.

"Matt! Can you walk?" Henry asked, his sandy blonde hair tousled and singed from the explosion. He offered me his hand, and with a surge of effort, I grabbed it, feeling the reassuring strength of my fellow pack mate as he helped me to my feet.

"Thanks," I grunted, wincing as pain lanced through my body. Despite the hurt, I knew we'd done what had to be done.

"Let's get to Lily," I said, the single-minded focus giving me the strength to push through the pain. As we limped away from the scene with the tactical team in tow, I knew there was still a long road ahead. But for now, at least, we had survived. And sometimes, survival was all we could hope for.

44

LILY JAMES

I woke up in a dimly lit room smelled of bleach and antiseptic. I knew I was in a hospital. Looking down at the crisp sheets and white blanket only confirmed my thoughts. The needle in my arm and the annoying beeping sounds coming from the machines around me left no room for denial. Despite my hatred for hospitals, being in one now seemed oddly comforting. It meant that I hadn't dreamt of being rescued and that, even just for now, I was safe.

Turning to my right, I saw Matt sitting in a chair next to the bed, his hand resting on mine. A smile crept onto my face, relieved knowing he was safe and here with me. I lay there staring at him, not wanting to wake him up. He looked so peaceful, and I wanted him to stay that way for a little while longer.

However, as if sensing my gaze, his eyes flicked open and met mine.

"Hey," I said, my voice hoarse and scratchy like it hadn't been used in a while.

"Hey," Matt whispered back, sitting up in the chair and

shifting it closer to me without releasing my hand. "How do you feel?" he asked, lifting my hand to his lips for a gentle kiss before placing it back on the bed.

"Sore and a bit tired," I replied. It felt as if sandpaper had been scraped against my throat for days, leaving it parched like the Sahara desert. Noticing my discomfort, Matt reached for the water jug and cup situated on the tray at the foot of my bed.

"Here, have some water," he suggested, pouring a glass for me and raising it to my mouth. Accepting it with both hands, I took a sip; the cool liquid was not just refreshing but also incredibly soothing to my throat.

"Thank you," I said to Matt, handing him the empty cup. He flashed me a smile and I returned it. "How long have I been here?" Curiosity overcame me.

"A few days," Matt replied, his face lined with worry as his brows furrowed.

"Days?" The word echoed in my mind. How had I been here for days when it felt like only a few hours?

"What do you remember?" Matt's expression was unreadable as he posed the question.

"I remember being kidnapped by my uncle, then the whipping," I responded, wincing at the lingering pain in my back. "Then you came to save me." Images of Matt finding me in that hellish place flashed through my mind, followed by another image of me shooting someone. Shocked by the recollection, I looked at Matt. "I shot someone," I confessed. "And you...you changed into your wolf form and you..."

"I killed your uncle," Matt finished for me. Then he fell silent, seemingly waiting for my reaction.

How did I feel about it? I asked myself. He was my uncle, someone I loved and admired for so many years. Even after everything that happened with my parents, he was still there for me. Then, to discover that he was the one actually responsible for all my sorrow and loss in the first place was devastating. Over the last few months, he had tormented and tortured me, killing more innocent people and making me feel accountable. The anger began to consume me, and I realised that I was relieved he was dead. Now, I could finally move on with my life without constantly looking over my shoulder wondering what would come next. "I'm glad you killed him," I told Matt honestly. "Now, I can finally move on with my life," I added as tears started streaming down my cheeks.

Matt rose from his chair and leaned in, planting a kiss on my forehead. "Yes, you can," he assured me, pulling back to rest his forehead against mine. At that moment, it felt as though a weight had been lifted off my shoulders. I sighed with relief, breathing in Matt's scent of fresh pine and mint that transported me back to the first time I laid eyes on him. It seemed as if even then, my soul knew we were destined for each other. At this very moment, I was certain that no matter what life hurled at us, we would weather it together.

"I love you, Matt," I confessed as I pulled away from him to look into his eyes.

"I love you too, Lilly," Matt responded, gracing me with the beautiful smile that I cherished so deeply.

"And I'm really going to love you later when I get out of here and recover from this," I hinted while gesturing towards my back.

Matt chuckled in response. "Oh, I very much look forward to that," he teased before winking at me and settling down on the bed beside me. He leaned in once more and sealed his promise with another kiss.

45

DETECTIVE MATTHEW ROCKLAN

Six weeks later, I found myself sitting in Sam's office, the weight of the investigation heavy on my shoulders. The report from the fire investigation department lay open before me, taunting me with its neatly typed words and official insignia. My eyes scanned the text, searching for some kind of solace.

"Damn bureaucracy," I muttered under my breath as the door to Sam's office swung open. In walked Sam, Miles, and Henry, their expressions a mixture of relief and exhaustion.

"Man, they're putting us through the wringer, huh?" Henry said, his sandy blonde hair tousled from running his hands through it a hundred times too many. At only 26, he was still a bit of a puppy in human years and shifter terms, but he could hold his own when it counted.

A collective sigh of relief filled the cramped office as Sam flipped through the final pages of the investigation report he had just received. I couldn't help but glance over at Henry, who nervously tapped his foot on the ground, a habit he picked up whenever he was anxious. Despite the formalities we had gone through, there was still an undeniable air of uncertainty lingering in the room.

"Alright, listen up," Sam began, his voice steady and authoritative. "The explosion has been ruled in our favor. The investigation showed that a stray bullet hit a gas cylinder and, combined with a faulty kitchen, caused the blast."

"Thank God," I muttered, feeling a weight lift off my shoulders.

"They couldn't find the location of the spark that ignited it all either," Sam continued. "The bodies were burned beyond recognition, and they were ruled to have died from the fire or some bullets from our police-issued guns."

"Does this mean we're in the clear?" Henry asked, his blue eyes wide with hope.

"Seems like it," Sam confirmed, a small smile tugging at the corner of his lips. "Looks like we can finally put this behind us."

I leaned back in my chair, a wave of relief washing over me. This was the last weight on my shoulder since getting Lily home. After much persuasion, I managed to convince her to quit her job, given the recovery time she needed to heal from the whipping and the time she had already taken off.

"Good riddance," I said, rubbing the back of my neck. "I just want to move on from all this."

"Me too," Henry agreed, his foot finally coming to a stop. "It's about time for some good news around here."

"Agreed," Sam nodded, closing the report and setting it aside.

"Here's to a fresh start," I said, feeling renewed hope.

With Lily safely home for the foreseeable future, my mind raced with plans to convince her to have my pups and become a traditional housewife. But deep down, I knew it was a futile attempt. She had already started pursuing job opportunities from our living room's comfort.

Hopefully, I can put a pup in her before she does. I have enough money to support us for a few years, and she has an inheritance from her parents and recently from her uncle. She's hesitated to use that money, but I thought it was a great opportunity and wanted to spend it all.

"Alright, Matt," Sam began, his voice calm and steady as he looked over the other documents on his desk. "I've got everything planned for the ceremony. It'll go ahead in three weeks."

"Fantastic," I replied, my voice cracking slightly under the weight of my nerves. I cleared my throat and continued, "I can't wait to show off my mate to the pack." A swarm of butterflies took flight in my stomach, their wings fluttering against my insides with anticipation and anxiety.

"Me too," said Sam, smiling warmly at me as he scratched his chin thoughtfully. "She's an amazing woman, Matt. I know the pack will love her as much as you do."

"Thanks, Sam," I murmured, feeling a sudden rush of gratitude for his support and friendship.

"Anyway," he continued, leafing through a folder, "the celebrant is all arranged so we can sign the paperwork after the ceremony. And the rings should be delivered soon."

"Rings?" I asked, quirking a brow in surprise. "I didn't think that was something our kind usually did."

"Usually not," he agreed, a mischievous twinkle in his eye. "But there's a new trend going around – silicone rings that stretch when we shift. So, Lily will get a beautiful diamond, and you'll get a simple silicone band."

"Wow," I breathed, my heart swelling with happiness at the thought of wearing something tangible to represent our union. "That's...that's perfect, Sam."

"Happy to help," he replied with a grin. "Now all that's left is for you to pop the question, mate."

My heart stuttered at his words, and I managed a weak laugh. "I know! I'm nervous, though."

"Come on," Sam chided gently, clapping me on the back. "She's your mate. It would be strange if she said no!"

"True," I chuckled, feeling more at ease now. "But stranger things have happened."

"Trust me," Sam advised, his eyes serious but warm. "You've got nothing to worry about. Just speak from the heart, and everything will fall into place."

He was right. If I spoke from the heart, Lily wouldn't say no. She couldn't.

"Thanks, Sam," I murmured, my voice thick with gratitude.

"No worries," he replied, his eyes sincere. "Now go on, get out of here, and ask that beautiful woman to marry you."

As I left his office, my heart pounding with anticipation and anxiety, I knew one thing for certain: I would do whatever it took to make Lily happy. And that started with the most important question of my life, which held the key to our future together.

Would she join me in our mating ceremony and marry me the same day…

46

LILY JAMES

Matt arrived home late in the afternoon. He entered through the front door, kicked off his shoes, and walked straight towards me. "How are you feeling?" he asked, wrapping his arms around me from behind as I stood at the kitchen bench making dinner.

"I should be asking you that question," I replied, relaxing back into his arms. He kissed my neck, and I tilted my head to the side to give him better access.

"I am great," Matt murmured between kisses. "You're home and recovering well; the investigation has been closed, and we can all sigh with relief."

Upon hearing those words, I put down the knife I was holding and turned in Matt's arms to face him. "It's over?" I asked, wrapping my arms around his neck. He pulled me closer to him, his body heat radiating against mine.

"It's finally over," Matt declared, grinning at me as relief washed over us. The investigation into the explosion had come to an end. Matt and his team were exonerated, allowing us to leave this ordeal in the past and move forward. I had been consumed by guilt when I discovered they were all under scrutiny because the explosion was deemed suspicious. Despite their assurances that it wasn't my burden to bear, I couldn't help but feel responsible; they were there for ME due to MY unhinged uncle. But now that it was all behind us, the sense of relief was overwhelming.

Matt pressed his forehead against mine, and we stood momentarily, breathing each other in. The calmness washed over us both through our connection. Each day, our bond grew stronger; it amazed me how we could sense each other's emotions without even being in the same room. Even though I wasn't a shifter, that factor didn't seem to hinder the strengthening of our connection. I pulled back and looked up at Matt, his love for me evident in his eyes as he peered into my soul. He leaned down and kissed me, which I welcomed. Matt licked my bottom lip, seeking access, and I granted it to him. Our tongues intertwined as we deepened the kiss. Our hands began exploring each other's bodies; Matt reached up between us and slipped his hand under my singlet, grasping my exposed breast.

"Hmm, I love it when you forgo your bra, allowing me full access," he murmured into my mouth, his fingers pinching my nipple and eliciting a moan from me. My body instinctively moved towards his touch. Matt broke our kiss and hoisted me onto the kitchen counter, parting my legs so he could position himself between them. He lifted my singlet over my head and tossed it haphazardly across the kitchen.

"Much better," he breathed out, leaning down to capture my right nipple with his mouth while caressing the left one with his hand.

"Ohh, Matt," I groaned as he alternated between sucking

and pinching my nipples, sending waves of excitement through me that made my toes curl in anticipation. He released my nipple with a pop and shifted his attention from right to left, each movement spurring further moans from me as I arched into him. I reached for the waistband of his pants but was met with a swift slap on my hand.

"You'll get your chance," he whispered, releasing my left nipple with an audible pop. I pouted at him, and he chuckled in response. Gently, he laid me back on the kitchen bench, drawing my legs towards him. Swiftly, he removed my shorts and panties, discarding them to join my singlet somewhere in the room. He parted my legs and took a deep breath. "God, I love your scent, Lily. It makes me incredibly hard," he confessed. His words stirred a pool of wetness within me; he made me feel like the most desirable woman alive. There was nothing more arousing than his current gaze - a deep lust filled his eyes as though he was about to devour me whole. He kept his eyes locked on mine as he lowered his head between my legs, lifting me slightly so that he could observe my reaction while his tongue explored my folds.

"Mmmmmm," I moaned, maintaining eye contact and licking my lips in anticipation. I was well aware of what that tongue was capable of, and the sight of him watching me had me all sorts of aroused. Then Matt dipped his tongue into my entrance. "Fuck," I moaned, encouraging him further. His slow and steady pace wasn't working for me, so I began to move my hips, but Matt used his hands to keep me still. I pouted at him, fully aware that he was teasing me on purpose, as he pulled back, eliciting a sigh of frustration from me. "You're quite eager, aren't you?" he breathed against my entrance while his tongue continued its tantalizing exploration.

"Matt, please," I pleaded, uncaring of the desperation lacing my voice. I wanted him, and I needed him immediately. Matt looked at me with a smirk, clearly enjoying my needy state. He rewarded my plea without further ado, lavishing attention on my clit as if he were a man starved.

"Matt..." I moaned out his name, praising the pleasure he was giving me. Just when I thought it couldn't get any better, he slipped two fingers inside me without warning.

"Oh God... Yes, Matt!" I cried out, arching my back as waves of intense pleasure coursed through me. Matt continued his ministrations unabated, his fingers pumping in and out while his mouth worked on my clit. The pressure built rapidly within me; I could feel how close I was to climaxing.

"Matt, I'm close," I announce, my body writhing as Matt continues his delicious assault. "Come for me, baby. Let me taste your sweetness," Matt says between licks and sucks. As if his words command my release, I go over the edge a few seconds later. My release rockets through me like a tidal wave; the pressure is so intense that my toes curl, and I scream Matt's name as my body trembles while Matt licks me gently as I ride out my orgasm.

As I come down, Matt pulls me off the bench, and before my feet even hit the floor, he spins me around, bending me over the bench and driving straight into me.

"Oh fuck, you're so wet for me," Matt moans out through gritted teeth as I let out a small moan loving how full I feel with him inside of me. He pulls back and rams into me again - deeper this time - making me clench.

"Fuck," Matt growls, his grip on my hips tightening as he thrusts into me with more force and speed. I adore it when he loses control like this, taking what he wants from me with a primal ferocity. With every thrust, Matt grunts, the sounds only making me even wetter. I can feel my arousal dripping out of me. Matt takes a deep breath and growls; I know he can smell how turned on I am, and it only spurs him to go even harder. He then releases one of my hips and moves his hand between my legs to find my swollen clit. He begins to stimulate the sensitive bud.

"Matt," I moaned, pushing back against him. I felt so sensitive and tender from my earlier orgasm. Matt was undeterred, continuing to rub my sensitive bud. "Come with me, Lily," he whispered into my ear, working my buds over time as he pumped in and out of me. Matt moaned as I began to clench around him, and I felt him begin to swell inside me. Seconds later, we were both moaning each other's names as we climaxed together. Matt collapsed on top of me, careful not to put all his weight on me. We stayed there like that, both panting and trying to catch our breaths.

"That was..." I started, but Matt interjected, completing my sentence with a summary. "Fucking perfection," he declared, planting a kiss on my shoulder as he withdrew from me. He then turned me to face him and enveloped me in his arms, our bare bodies pressed together.

A satisfied smile spread across my face as I looked up at him, feeling content and fulfilled. Matt hoisted me up, and I instinctively wrapped my legs around his waist as he began moving us towards the bedroom.

"Where are we heading?" I queried, nuzzling into his neck.

"Dessert time," Matt announced, giving my bottom a playful slap as he quickened his pace towards the bedroom.

"Hmm, dessert," I murmured into his neck before teasingly licking it. "This time, it's my turn to make you beg," I warned him playfully, lifting my head to arch an eyebrow at him while winking suggestively.

"Oh, I'll beg for you any day of the week," Matt retorted with a smirk, mirroring my wink. Laughter bubbled up within me as anticipation for what was about to unfold set in.

I knew I shouldn't be doing this, but I couldn't help myself. The flashing blue and red lights on the dashboard of my car gave me a sense of urgency as I sped through the streets. I had to get to where I was going – fast. Sam would surely forgive me for this little transgression, right?

I focused on weaving through traffic, pushing my car to its limits. My heart raced, partly from the adrenaline of driving like a maniac but mostly because of where I was headed.

A grin spread across my face as I swerved in and out, running through red lights and racing down the streets. My heart pounded in my chest, a strange mix of adrenaline and pure happiness coursing through my veins.

As I continued my wild ride, I couldn't help but marvel at the changes in my life over the past four years. Who would have thought I'd end up mated, married, and head over heels in love? Certainly not me, that's for sure.

"Four years ago, I never would've believed I'd be where I am now," I muttered, glancing at the wedding band on my finger. The simple black silicone band symbolized the incredible journey I'd been on since meeting Lily.

Some say that fate brings you to the one you are meant to be with, and that was certainly true for me. She charged into my life like a tornado, leaving a trail of chaos and love in her wake. The day we first met will forever be ingrained in my memory as the moment my life changed for the better. And when she let me mark her as mine, it further solidified our bond. Our mating ceremony was a celebration of love and unity, and today, as I watch her prepare to welcome our first pup into the world, I couldn't be more grateful for the journey she has taken me on. She is my soulmate, and I can't wait to see our future.

I cut the lights as I parked in the designated police parking at the front of the hospital, again a big no-no, but I'll ask Sam for forgiveness later. Stepping out of the car, I felt my heart pounding against my chest like a caged animal fighting to be free. A cool breeze brushed against my face, and the scent of antiseptic and anxiety filled the air.

"Get it together, Matt," I muttered as I raced inside. The sterile white walls and fluorescent lights did nothing to calm my nerves, but I knew I had to keep moving. I was a man on a mission – Lily needed me.

"Excuse me!" I shouted, pushing past people as I approached the lift. "Coming through!"

"Watch it, buddy!" a nurse snapped as I nearly barrelled into her, but I barely had time to apologize before the doors closed, whisking me away to the maternity ward. As the lift ascended, I leaned against the wall to steady my breathing.

"Okay, Matt, you got this," I told myself, feeling my palms grow sweaty. "You're about to meet your first pup. ...breathe."

When the doors finally opened, I practically leaped into the hallway, following the signs to the maternity ward. Her water had broken while out on her run today, three weeks early, I might add, but she had managed to call for an ambulance to transfer her to the hospital.

I had been crouched behind a stack of crates in an abandoned warehouse, with the scent of damp and decay thick in my nostrils, straining to hear the hushed voices of Matteo Ricci and his goons. But my phone buzzed in my pocket.

"Matt," Lily's voice came through, breathless and scared. "It's time."

Time seemed to stop momentarily as her words echoed in my head, drowning out the sinister murmurs of the mafia men just feet away from me. My hand tightened around the phone, my mind racing with a million thoughts simultaneously. The baby couldn't wait. I had to get to Lily now.

"Stay there, babe. I'm on my way," I whispered urgently, ignoring the cold sweat prickling at my neck as I extricated myself from my hiding spot and bolted out of the warehouse.

My instincts sharpened to razor-fine points as I tracked Lily's scent through the maze of sterile corridors and bustling nurses.

Finally, I found her room. The door stood slightly ajar, and her scent - a mix of fear, pain, and the unmistakable musk of a wolf pup - engulfed me like a tidal wave. My legs felt weak, but I forced myself to stand tall as I pushed open the door and stepped inside.

"Hey," I said softly, my voice cracking with emotion as I took in the sight of Lily lying in the hospital bed, her face flushed and damp with sweat. "Sorry, I'm late."

"Nice of you to join me, Mr. Rocklan," she said, her voice

weak but full of teasing warmth. My heart swelled with love for this incredible woman.

"Hey, how're you doing? How's the baby?" I asked, leaning down to kiss her lips gently.

"Sweetheart, we still have ages," she chuckled, which was music to my ears. I'm only 1 cm dilated, and the contractions are far apart. The midwife suggested I get up and walk around, but I wanted to wait for you.

"Of course, my dear, anything for you," I replied, smiling at her determination. "Let me help your 'whale body' off the bed so we can walk."

"Very funny," she rolled her eyes, but her laughter told me she appreciated the light-hearted banter. As a shifter, lifting her was no issue; she felt as light as a feather in my arms. I held out my arm gallantly, playing the part of the gentleman escort.

"Would you do me the honor, Mrs. Rocklan, and accompany me on this walk?" I asked, trying to inject some fun into the situation.

"Yes, sir, I would!" she responded playfully, gently punching my arm. Together, we walked the hospital corridors, hand in hand. Our connection deepened with each step, and anticipation built within me.

And just like that, hours later, we welcomed our first baby girl pup, a precious bundle of joy named Charlie Rocklan. Life would never be the same, but I knew we were ready to embrace this new journey together.

The End

About Cassandra Doon

Cassandra Doon hails from New South Wales, Australia, where she was nurtured between the bustling streets of Sydney and the serene snowy mountains of Tumut. Today, she finds inspiration in the breathtaking Scenic Rim of Queensland's Gold Coast. A versatile author with a lifelong passion for storytelling, Cassandra has penned over 16 novels and 5 children's books, exploring a variety of genres. Known for her daydreaming and a head often lost in the clouds, she admits to being more at home in her fictional worlds than on social media. Outside of her literary pursuits, Cassandra is a devoted mother to two boys, dedicating her days to their endless energy as both a soccer mom and Pokémon master.

Join her Facebook readers Group:
https://www.facebook.com/groups/1113426753355119/

Or follow on Instagram:
https://www.instagram.com/cassandradoonauthor

ALSO CASSANDRA DOON

The 4 Seats Series:

Matteo

Felix

Gabe (Coming Soon)

Catcher

Ruhn & Frost (Coming Soon)

Standalone:

The Boys Of Hastings House
The Kings of Willows Peak
Damaged Goods
Tuesday May
The Devils Cut
The Detectives Mate
Bittersweet Snapdragon
The Dead Zone (Coming Soon)
Second Chances at The Riverbend Café (Coming Soon)
Still Waters (Coming Soon)
Aces (Coming Soon)
Lavender (Coming Soon)
Dark Dahlia Rite (Coming Soon)
Shadow Prince (Coming Soon)
Ravenwood Manor (Coming Soon)
Summer (Coming Soon)

Oakland Harbour Series:

Missing
Found
Home

Second Chances Series:

The Waterfall
Wicked Bonds (Coming Soon)
The Restaurant (Coming Soon)

Haunted Tales and Withered Old Flowers Series:

A Field of Tulips and Bones (Coming Soon)
Muddy White Lillies (Coming Soon)

The Queens of Shadows Series:

Follow Poppy
Protecting Poppy (Coming Soon)
Crowning Poppy (Coming Soon)

About Casey Rolls

Casey Rolls is an Australian writer who writes Romance, fantasy and shifter stories. She was raised between Queensland and New South Wales, with a childhood spent on the water and anything the water had to offer. Now residing on the Gold Coast in Queensland, she lives a hectic life working full time and looking after her daughter, but she lets her imagination take over at night. Her writing is heavily influenced by her interest in the supernatural world and her desire to create the perfect love story with all the drama along the way.

ALSO CASEY ROLLS

Standalone:

The Detectives Mate
Bittersweet Snapdragon
Not anyone's Dirty secret (Coming Soon)